CAGING ELLA

DARK AND TWISTED FAIRY TALES

ANDIE M. LONG

For the words that speared my caged psyche until I let them free.

Caging Ella

A paranormal fairy tale re-telling... of vampires, captivity, and love.

They said that *Once Upon a Time*, Cinderella resided with her monstrous stepmother, ugly stepsisters, and led a life of cruel drudgery, until one day, a fairy godmother helped her attend a ball, where she met a charming prince and lived happily ever after.

But what if he was a dark prince? A vampire? And Ella the daughter of his maid? What if he wanted Ella to birth his children? Could not wait for a taste of her sweet chaste desire...

After six years of captivity with her cruel father and stepfamily, will Ella wish to be free, or will she tie herself to Beau for eternity?

CHAPTER 1

ELLA

The news of my mother's death was delivered to me as I scrubbed the kitchen floor, like it was another chore issued from my stepmother's mouth.

My knees were aching, and no doubt bruised from being knelt on the flagstone for so long, and my back felt broken. My chapped, and wrinkled fingered hand dropped the scrubbing brush back into the bucket as her feet, shoes still on, walked across the clean portion, her stride purposeful. I swiped a hand through my dirty blonde hair, cleaning the sweat from my brow as I did so, then sat back on my heels and looked at her. What had I done wrong this time? Because I'd always done *something* wrong.

I met her intense stare. Took in the smirk on her face. The false smile before the sharp tongue struck out. I imagined that she slithered upon the ground. Her tongue forked. Her body wrapping around my neck and pulling tight.

"Oh, Ella, Ella, Ella." She shook her head, then tilted it toward me. "My poor child. I just came to tell you that if you still believed your mother was going to save up enough money to go to court and get you away from us, it's not going to happen now, seeing as she's dead."

The words hit me as hard as any slap against my face ever could have.

Dead.

Dead.

Dead. Dead. Dead.

"*No!*" I backed away from her, my knees soaking in the residue. My hand to my mouth as I gasped for air.

No, no, no, no, no.

"Glennis!" my father yelled from the hall before appearing in the doorway. His eyes looked upon me.

Daddy, please, I need you.

"You could have waited until she'd finished the floor."

I felt the ricochet of his words *finished the floor, finished the floor*. Even death didn't humanise my father. Standing up, feeling like someone had shot me at close range, I fled the room, careful to avoid my father in the doorway. As I passed him, I heard his words to my stepmother, "See, now the floor's still filthy."

She's dead.

She's dead.

She's dead. Dead. Dead.

I placed my hands over my ears as if I could block out my stepmother's vengeful words.

Somehow, my feet carried me to the steps of the cellar, where I threw myself upon the single mattress I called my bed. It hurt due to its thinness, the hard floor underneath seeming to soak through and meet my bones, but I didn't care. I couldn't have hurt any more than I did right now if someone had broken me apart one bone at a time. My body felt weak, and I swore my heart wasn't beating right because it was now broken. My mother—my beautiful, sweet mother—was gone. How? What had happened? I'd only spoken to her a few short days ago. She'd been in good spirits. So excited about my upcoming eighteenth birthday. Promising me that my patience at waiting for her was about to be rewarded.

I felt like an angel had lifted me up to the sky, had

shown me the whole of the earth that was at my finger-tips, and then a devil had knocked me from their hands.

To witnesses, I was laid on a hard mattress in a basement. To an empath, I was destroyed. Smashed to smithereens. Bones broken, guts leaching out, my heart shot to pieces.

I rubbed at my chest, then coughed, needing to try to get my heart to beat properly. I was so dizzy. Nauseous. I kept swallowing, feeling like my throat was constricted.

She's dead.

She's dead.

She's dead. Dead. Dead.

My mother was dead, and now I was stuck here, maid to my father, stepmother, and two stepsisters, until such time as I could afford to escape. And I knew my stepmother would never let that happen. I was too useful as her servant. I cooked, cleaned, and stayed out of the way, and in return I could eat the leftovers, and have a mattress in the cellar. Mice and spiders were my only company.

It had been a long time since I'd allowed myself to feel any emotion. For many years I'd bottled all my reactions deep inside myself, the constant lump in my throat the cork that stoppered my true feelings from spilling out.

But now I allowed myself to picture my mother at her best. Back before my father had cheated on her and thrown her out penniless, and she'd had to take the cleaning job over at Moonstone Castle. The job no one else wanted as the man who lived in the large castle was rumoured to be a mean, nasty individual who hated people, and the castle so large it was impossible for one person to keep on top of things as he demanded.

How had our lives changed so much?

Simple. Because of my father's wandering eye and my stepmother's calculating ones.

Tears spilled down over my lashes, and an anguished sob escaped me as all the hope I'd had soaked into the thin bedlinen below me.

I gave myself five minutes. Once my watch reached five fifteen, I dragged myself from the mattress, and washed my face in the bucket of cold water I kept in the corner of the room. Returning upstairs, I cleaned the floor, starting from the beginning. There was a whole evening of tasks to be done and my mother's death had excused me from none of them.

When the clock struck midnight that was my time to myself. I snuck out of the house, the rest of them all fast asleep in their comfortable beds, content due to the gluttony of their lives. Fixing my black trench coat around myself against the chill and damp in the air, I pulled the back door closed and walked down the street until I reached the park. My coat and shoes were designer, given to me in case I was seen out in public. The only concession from my stepmother, who the rest of the time delighted in giving me ill-fitting thread-bare jogging suits she'd acquired from God only knew where. I had one dress that had been my mother's. It too was worn and bore holes. But the emerald-green maxi fitted me like a glove now. I smoothed a hand down the material. The dress a connection between me and my dear mum.

The night was still and silent, yet dark and menacing at the same time. The trees cast their shadows like waiting monsters, and the stormy night sky meant the park itself was barely visible other than the soft glow of the streetlamps that marked the path-ways. I set off down the path, finding a bench donated by the relatives of a passed on beloved grandmother, and dropped down onto it. Here in the dark, I wasn't afraid, because I'd left the real monsters behind, back where I lived. I saw nothing to fear in the cool, damp air and the darkness. To me it was the only time I could breathe.

I let my thoughts consume me. Let my mind wander back to my mother.

Had she managed to save any money at all, or had it all been lies to keep me hoping?

Would some inheritance be coming my way, no matter how small? I could buy some new material, make myself some new clothes, get a new mattress. Anything to improve on what I had now.

I sighed. Anything sent my way would be intercepted by my father. I'd never see a penny of it. He was always saying my mother owed him for the luxurious life she'd had before he'd discarded her like a broken umbrella.

Twelve-year-old me had hidden behind a door listening to his cruel words on the night he'd thrown her out and moved his mistress and her children in. Before this, he'd been an absent father who was always working. My mother made excuses on his behalf, saying he'd be with me if he could but that he was out providing for us. I'd believed her. Thought him a hero for his sacrifice that meant I had a room full of toys and a wardrobe of pretty dresses. That night I began to learn the truth of who my father was...

．　．　．

"Grant, listen to reason. Okay, you're done with me. You own the house and so I know I've no choice but to leave. But I want my daughter. She's everything to me. You've never been bothered about her, so why are you insisting she stays now? You have Glennis and her two daughters. Please, Grant. I won't go to court for any divorce settlement if you'll be reasonable and just let me take Ella. You can see her when you want, but I beg you, let me take Ella."

I heard her strangled cry of frustration, followed by his bark of laughter.

"I'm done with you, Freya. You've served your purpose. Ella is my heir, though I hope to find someone better than the pathetic girl you've raised who thinks she's a princess and that some handsome prince is going to drive up to the house in a Bugatti and swear his undying love. She stays and I'm going to teach her real life. That sometimes you have to get your hands dirty."

"Then I'll have no choice than to get dirty myself and fight you in court. I'll use my half of our money."

He chuckled unpleasantly. "Do you think I got to where I am in life by letting anyone get the upper hand? Our marriage wasn't legal, darling. There is no half for you. You're entitled to nothing. And with that nothing you have no money to go to any courts. Ella stays with me." He was relishing the conversation. His voice boastful, and cruel.

"Y-you're lying. We are married."

"Do I look like I'm lying? You were a prize when I met you, your father so happy to take me onto the board of his emerging acquisitions empire. But I acquired you **and** his business."

"My father left you his business because he loved you." My mum spoke softly, her voice a plea for him to see reason.

"Your father had his heart attack because I drove him to it."

"No."

One simple word, that cracked as she spoke it, and broke my mother along with it. The cheating hurt, my father's betrayal stung, but learning he'd driven her father to his death crushed my mother. Adding that she was now penniless and couldn't have custody of me drove his boot in further.

I stepped out from behind the door.

"I want to be with my mum," I yelled, running to

her. Those arms I'd always known I could count on opened for me to run to her and cling on tight.

But my father's rough grip held me back. I bore the marks of his fingertips for days.

"Your place is here, Ella, and if you go to the living room quietly, I'll let your mother contact you once a week. Otherwise, you'll never hear from her again."

"Mum!"

She straightened herself and looked at me kindly, "My dear Ella. I will earn and save money and return for you. Stay strong, my darling daughter." She blew me a kiss and I pretended to catch it and placed it on the top of my head. The place my mother smelled my hair and kissed when telling me she loved me... loved the very bones of me.

"Go," my father ordered, and I wasn't sure if he meant me or my mother. We both left anyway. The invisible biological thread between us tearing and hurting as we became further apart.

My new stepmother and stepsisters were in the living room, and when my father returned, I was told how things would be from now on. That I'd start as he did from the bottom up. Learn to appreciate and earn my rewards in life. But as the years passed, he forgot all that. He decided to sell the company and enjoy the wealth he'd earned. He stayed on as a consultant. His wife and *her children busied themselves with the activities of the wealthy: salon visits, shopping trips.*

While I kept the house tidy and all but disappeared from his memories. No longer a daughter, an heir, but a servant. No rewards for hard work, like new shoes or ice cream, or his admiration. I hated that I'd wanted his praise.

And my stepmother stripped me of everything as soon as he stopped looking: my belongings other than the dress and watch I refused to give up, and my dignity.

Now I wondered if he'd tried to drive my mother to her death too. But while she'd had hope, could save up, and one day come for me, she'd kept going. As my father had promised, I'd been allowed one phone call with her a week, on a Friday evening. Ten minutes where she told me about the castle she worked in, about a different room she'd cleaned and the beautiful things she'd found there. I'd lie and tell her about how well I was being looked after. How beautiful my own room was. She'd end every call with, "I love you, Ella Louise, and soon I'll be able to fight for shared custody, I promise."

But it had never happened.

And I was never sure why. It was almost six years

later. Six years of working in the castle. She'd enjoyed the work, loved the building, and now, one week away from my eighteenth birthday, she was gone.

"A pretty girl like you shouldn't be out all alone in the dark," a male voice said, startling me, my brain hurtling through time back to the present moment, a small gasp leaving my mouth.

CHAPTER 2

ELLA

I leapt to my feet in a Taekwondo back stance, placing a healthy distance between us, my arms up in readiness to defend myself.

"A pretty girl like me should be able to do whatever I damn well like," I spat out, angry at the fact he'd made me jump and interrupted me from thoughts of my dear mother. "It's the ones who prey on us who shouldn't be out. *They* should be locked up."

"A fair point," the man said, his voice clear and precise. "My apologies. I didn't mean to startle you. I was just concerned to see you out alone so late and looking so... lost. But you're right. If we live in a world of equality, I should not bother asking you if you're okay, thinking of you as a potentially vulnerable female. Nor should I comment on the facial features of yours I find quite delightful. I should instead leave you well alone and mind my business. Good evening."

I stared at him, bewildered by his weird conversation. He was tall, with dark wavy hair that had a little salt and pepper at the roots. His eyes were dark, and I couldn't make out the colour in the limited visibility. His skin was pale, although warmed by the light of the streetlamp. He moved to turn away.

"A world of equality," I scoffed, placing my hands on my hips, yet keeping a good distance between us. "I find I'm yet to experience such a world, *sir*."

His lip quirked. "I'm sure you'll do your best to rectify that. You have a certain, *manner* about you. Anyway, I wish you all the very best. Enjoy the rest of your evening, and if you hear me scream, I'd appreciate it if you'd come rescue *me* in this brave new world where the tides are changing. Though." He tapped his lip. "What if I'm just yelling out in the throes of passion because I've hooked up with someone in the park? That would be rather embarrassing."

His cadence continued to be a teasing dance; each word strung together like the weave of a feather boa across my senses. Despite his strangeness, he'd piqued my curiosity.

"It is you who should think of their safety then, if that's what you're out seeking this evening."

He arched a brow. "You think hook-ups are risqué?"

"No, I just hope you have condoms. Because otherwise the risk is you get a disease, or you get a child you treat as a disease. Better the potential ends up in a litter bin."

"You are very bitter for one so young."

"And you are very strange for whatever age you are."

He laughed then. "You're right. I am. I am very strange. And I won't be screaming in passion in the park because I am actually saving my seed for the right person to carry my children. Can you believe that? When you look upon me, do I seem like someone who would want to do things right?"

Who spoke like this? And why was I carrying on a conversation with a weirdo I should have told to go away by now? There was just something about him. Maybe the fact he was letting me have an opinion. Was listening to me. Dismissing my thoughts, I shrugged. "People show their true faces and still you can't tell the monsters from the good guys," I said. "When I look upon you, I cannot decide whether you are a psychopath playing with me before you murder me, someone bored who is amusing themselves at my expense, or someone in need of a straitjacket."

"I'll give you a clue. I'm kind of all three."

"And what do you see, when you look upon me?" I asked him, because as weird as this evening had gotten, he was distracting me from my grief, albeit temporarily.

"Hmmm." He looked me up and down but stared far longer at my face than my body. "I see someone who life has made hard as stone. There's a crack there with light trying to seep out, but here you are in the darkness, resisting letting it break further open."

"I think I'd like to be alone again now," I said dismissively, because he was too close to the truth.

"You don't always have to hide in the darkness, you know?" he added. "The moon comes out so you can shine in it too. Goodnight, Ella," he said.

"What did you say?" I snarled, ready to face off with him again.

His upper lip quirked. "I said goodnight, *bella*. I spent some time in Italy recently. I guess I should have said it properly, *buonanotte bella*. My apologies that I called you a beauty though. It is hard to break the habit of compliments."

"It's not appropriate," I said, though my brain was still recovering from the fact I'd thought he'd known my name.

He shrugged his shoulders. "Why deny what you are, *uno freddo*?"

"What's Italian for creep?" I shot back.

He laughed and strode away, walking further into the park. Once he'd gone from sight, I picked up my phone and Googled uno freddo.

The translation appeared—cold one.

Yes, I much preferred that to being called beautiful.

CHAPTER 3

BEAU

Six years ago...

No one stayed long at Moonstone Castle. The work was too hard, the pay too low, and the boss too miserable and rarely available. It wasn't my fault I couldn't come out until dark. That large annoyance was entirely due to my sire, whom I'd last seen when he'd been murdered in the castle around thirty years ago. I'd loved every minute of plunging the stake through his selfish heart. In fact, I regretted my impulsive action because he was dusted in a flash, and I'd learned I'd enjoyed the power I'd wielded for that sliver of time.

Free of him, I had adored my solitude. However,

the staff had eventually left as I had nothing to pay them with, and the castle had fallen into a state of disrepair and grime.

Every so often I advertised for someone to house-keep, but either I disliked them intensely and they left due to my sharp tongue (never my teeth though it was often tempting), or they found the job too taxing. I survived on drinking the blood delivered in bags monthly, or if especially tight on available finances, from the animals who lived in the acres of land surrounding the castle and all was satisfactory.

Until one day a knock came to the door that would change things. Change me.

The darkness had fallen, and the hour had passed eleven, so the sound of the knocker was unexpected. So much so that even I, a bloodsucker, checked through the spyhole.

Human.

A human female, tired, and shoulders hunched.

I was pleased I'd fed well that evening.

The door creaked as I opened it, and I mentally cursed the fact that my home had slowly turned into a stereotypical house of horrors.

The woman's eyes widened as she stared at me. "I-I'm sorry to bother you this late on an evening."

"It's no bother. Are you all right? Lost?"

She swallowed. To my superior hearing her nerves and agitation were plain to note.

She stood up straighter. "I'm looking for a job and heard you had need of a housekeeper."

"I do," I said. "Would you like to come inside and interview?"

The woman nodded. "If it's not too late."

I opened the door wider. "I work at night. I prefer it. So for me the day has just started. Please come inside. You look exhausted. Did you walk all the way from the entrance?"

"I walked all the way from my previous home, in Poplar."

I gave her a weak smile. "That's quite some distance," I offered in a kindly tone.

"I may as well be honest. Desperation carried me here. My circumstances have changed in the blink of an eye." A tear bloomed on her right lower lash as she spoke.

"Come in. Let's not keep you standing out here any longer. I have what I've been told is a comfy sofa."

She followed me inside, her eyes taking in every cobweb, every piece of furniture. I took her into the best sitting room that I'd attempted to keep moderately clean and gestured to the sofa, while I went to my drinks cabinet.

"I can't make you a hot beverage because I don't think I have a single item in date and certainly no milk, but I can offer you a scotch or a port?"

"I'll take a port, thank you. I feel I deserve it," she answered.

Though I usually despised company, I found myself fascinated by the slight, fragile looking human woman who'd had the inner strength and outer persistence to walk all the way to my door to ask for a job. I poured her a decent measure and did the same for myself. Passing her the glass, I settled into the chair opposite.

"Let's get introductions out of the way, shall we, and air our truths? I'm Beau Salinger. I inherited this house some years ago, but I struggle to afford to keep it running. However, I love the place and so refuse to sell it either. It means I cannot offer much pay, but you can take up whichever of the rooms you'd like on the west side of the building. The work is keeping the home as clean as possible and alerting me to anything that might need urgent repair, though I'm aware the house is vast and too much for one person. Just do what you can. I have no need of drinks or meals. I'm very self-sufficient in some regards. I enjoy keeping my strange hours and much *prefer to be up while it's dark and asleep when it's light. I have a skin complaint which makes me sensitive to the sun."*

"I thought we were speaking our truths," the woman said.

I frowned. "I'm not sure I understand what you're alluding to."

She straightened in her seat, and met my gaze with confidence, her head slightly tilted. "You are awake at night, don't need human food or drink, and are sensitive to the sun. You are a vampire. Or am I mistaken and foolish to believe in such things?"

I spluttered out my port.

"While you decide what to tell me further, I'll take my turn. I'm Freya Story. My husband just threw me out of my marital home to move in his mistress and her two daughters instead. He then told me we were never married, and he'd been with me to steal my father's business. He has our daughter. Ella. She's twelve. He wouldn't allow me to take her with me, and so I need a job and a place to stay. My intentions were to save enough to fight for custody, though I know that won't be easy. He is a powerful man. However, knowing you cannot pay me much, I would like to negotiate a different form of payment."

I placed my chin in my hand. "Go on."

"I will keep this place, and your secret..."

I began to protest, but she held up a hand.

"I've never heard of anything more than one man being in this castle for years. And now I've seen you for myself... I'm not a fool."

I nodded. "May I enquire of how you know about vampires?"

She nodded. "My mother had the sight, and along with it she told me of many things beyond the realm of what others believed in. In the end it drove her mad. I did not inherit the sight, but I never doubted the things my mother told me. It was only being unable to control the voices of the spirits that tormented her into taking her own life."

"I'm sorry."

"It was a long time ago now but thank you."

For a moment there was a pause in conversation until I realised Freya was waiting for me to speak.

"Okay, back to what you were saying... You'll keep both the house and my secret..."

"And you will pay me whatever you can afford. But in addition, you will keep an eye on Ella for me. Because my husband will not let me near her. Then, when she is eighteen and able to be legally free of him, you will bring her here. To me."

"I could just go and bleed him dry tonight. No one would ever know," I offered.

Freya shook her head. "She's in a wealthy home. She can receive what I cannot give her right now. My husband may be ruthless, but I know when I'm beaten. He said he intended for her to not be so pampered, but I believe that was just to belittle my parenting. As his heir, he will wish to give her a good education. So for the next few years, I will do whatever is necessary for Ella to continue that education. Then once we bring her here at eighteen, we may make plans for the future. I will sacrifice my time with my daughter now, knowing that in the end it will be better. Yes, that's what I think right now is the best option for her, for my Ella Louise. What do you say? Do we have an agreement?"

"You're committing to over six years here. What if you hate it?"

She spoke with passion. "I will always love my daughter more than I will hate anything or anyone. That's why despite my present feelings for her father, I am considering her best interests. Do you need to draw up a contract? I'm ready to sign."

"If we shake on it, you'll be bound to me and our agreement," I warned her. "To your service here as a housekeeper, and my promise to keep an eye on Ella, and bring her here to you at eighteen." I held out my hand.

She leaped up and shook it.

"It is done," I said.

"Excellent. Now could you show me the most urgent rooms that need to be cleaned and then where I may sleep?" she requested. Her body language had changed since we'd made our deal. Her shoulders now relaxed, and a determination evident in her expression.

She followed me out to the hall, and we walked to the kitchen. She began to look amused as she took in the dust-laden table and countertops. "It would appear it has been a while since you had visitors."

"Other than my food delivery and other business, it has been left since my last housekeeper quit."

"Then in the morning, I will clean and throw out anything no longer of use," she said as she walked around opening and closing cupboards.

"You may want to purchase an apron so as not to ruin that pretty dress," I said, because she'd come to me in desperation, but her attire smacked of wealth.

"As I said earlier, my life has changed completely. However, I never let my advantages in life change who I was inside. It is but fabric, and I shall in time buy more and make myself everything I need. It will keep me busy in my spare hours."

This woman impressed me more and more by the minute. Something in her refusal to give in despite what life was throwing at her was waking something within myself. Maybe I had festered too long in this castle and needed to also be open to a fresh perspective?

"There is material around this castle. Old curtains and tablecloths etc. Organise what is needed for the castle and feel free to use anything which remains," I told her.

"Thank you."

From there we walked back through the hallway and I stopped at the foot of the stairs. "This also needs cleaning if you could. The windows are filthy and again the place is thick with dust.

"I shall get it back to its best," she said.

"Thank you. Now if you follow me I will show you your rooms."

We walked up the vast staircase, her keeping one step behind me and I stopped at the top, waiting until she came alongside me.

"My suite of rooms is that way," I explained, *pointing to the right. Then I turned left, walking down until I reached the first door.*

Opening it revealed a suite of rooms. "This is what I suggest you use, although feel free to change to any of the others on this hallway."

She looked around. "This will be perfect. Thank you."

"It is getting late for a human so I will bid you goodnight," I said. "I will be in my office if you need me. That's down the hall, first door on the right."

"Thank you, Mr Salinger."

I shook my head. "Beau."

She smiled. "Thank you, Beau. We shall talk some more after dark tomorrow, when I've had a good look around. Just for your information, I will be warding myself and the room for this evening and beyond. My mother taught me what to do."

I arched a brow. "You don't trust me?"

"Given what my husband just did to me, it will be a miracle if I ever trust anyone again," she said firmly. "Yet my instincts tell me that despite the rumours, you are a good man. However, I don't trust the thirst, so I'll err on the side of caution."

"Wise. I have wards on my bedroom too. No one can enter while I am asleep."

"You expect enemies to come?" her words came fast with a hint of anxiety.

I shook my head. "Just scared of monsters."

She laughed then. Years fell from her as she did so. And that was when a strange friendship began, between a human female and an introverted male vampire.

. . .

But while she kept the place clean and suggested ways to earn the money for repairs, dealing with selling objects and paintings she found around the place, I ended up keeping secrets from Freya, as it was better to do so.

Because when I went to see Ella, after dusk, I could find no trace of her scent while outside of the bedroom windows. Eventually, the small window in the cellar, there for nothing more than ventilation and giving barely any light, revealed the girl's living arrangement. I could never see her, but I paid someone to hack into her computers where her father had her doing her education online. She was bright, and she'd been spending the little time she had before sleep learning Taekwondo. During the winter when dusk fell early and I could get out, I hung around outside and heard her family order her around. She was treated like a servant, not a daughter. But they didn't harm her physically, and I saw the strength blooming within the young girl. The wiliness.

And once a week when her mother called her, Ella told her how wonderful her life was, keeping her mother happy, though she asked every week how her mother's savings were going because she wanted to be with her.

There was nothing I could do. Or maybe I just chose not to.

Because revealing the truth may have resulted in Freya's panic for her daughter. To her demanding she be brought here to my castle. Then what? I couldn't have the drama brought to my door, so what would I do? Drain the family and bring Ella here? At twelve years old, with her father, new wife, and stepsisters murdered. Finding herself in a strange house where she'd see her mother still couldn't help her. No savings, no prospects, no decent education. A twelve-year-old didn't belong here.

No, it was better to leave her, to watch her become strong and resilient, until her eighteenth birthday. Then I'd bring her to her mother, and they could move on.

Except the girl was now one week from her eighteenth birthday and her mother had died.

I could forget all about Ella Louise Story and attempt to find a new housekeeper.

Or I could fulfil her mother's wishes and bring her here to her. To her grave. I could tell her about her mother and offer her a job until she got on her feet.

I figured that was the least I could do, for my dear friend Freya.

Which was why—with one week to go until her eighteenth birthday—when I saw her in the park, this time I decided to speak to her. To come out of the shadows... and to embrace the ones that surrounded her.

CHAPTER 4

ELLA

I woke having had tormented dreams: my mother at my window, face etched in panic, begging me to help her. Me unable to open the window and then her falling to her death. I wasn't in my cellar bedroom, but my old one in the attic. The one where I'd thought my life was perfect.

It meant there wasn't even a minute of peace where my mother wasn't dead. No stillness in the space between being still half asleep and then being awake. Just separating dream death from reality. As I got off my mattress, I didn't bother to look at myself or to wash my face. I just dressed back in my cleaning clothes of a grey sweater and jogging bottoms and made my way upstairs to begin my morning chores. I was beginning to think life had leached out of me too. Like I was a grey sky holding onto stormy rainclouds, wallowing in my misery instead of letting it out in a burst of thunderous precipitation.

As I opened the curtains it seemed the day had decided to join me. I had to put the lights on as it was so dull.

In the kitchen, I began to prepare all the different breakfasts the household demanded, and while I did, I thought of the strange man from last night. It was my hope that I wouldn't bump into him again. I liked the space my walks provided me with. The solitude. If the park became the weirdo's walk too, then I'd be lost. There was nothing else like it around here.

I thought about Moonstone Castle where my mother had worked and died. The gothic castle surrounded by woods. I only knew it from my mother's descriptions on the phone, but it seemed the perfect place for a walk if the owner hadn't always kept it all to himself. One day I would like to live in a home of my own with a garden for myself.

Fury hit me out of nowhere.

Boiling red rage of the hand dealt to me.

I let the plate I was holding slip from my hand and crash to the floor where it broke into three separate pieces.

My stepmother burst into the kitchen. "What is all

the noise, Ella? I've only just woken up." She looked at the floor.

"You stupid clumsy bitch. That was my favourite plate. In fact, I think you broke that on purpose." Her eyes narrowed. "Pick the pieces up then, you idiot," she yelled.

I dropped to my haunches and picked up the three pieces.

"Hand them over," Glennis demanded.

My brow creased, but I did as she asked. Her shoulders shook in anger as she looked over the pieces of a plate I used in rotation with many others. Not anything I'd ever heard mention of being her favourite until now I'd broken it.

"I will find more jobs for you to do until you've earned enough money to replace this," she said. "Now dispose of it carefully." I held out my hand and Glennis slammed the pieces down into it, with the sharp points facing my palm. Two broke through my skin, puncturing the flesh, and I winced and cried out.

"So careless today. For goodness' sake, hurry up and get the breakfast out. We have busy days ahead of us all."

She bustled out of the room, and I put the broken pieces in the bin and looked at my hand where the blood bloomed. It hurt, but what hurt more was it was the first time Glennis had caused me a physical injury. Mental abuse, yes. Physical abuse from all the chores, yes. But she'd refrained from injuring me before now. It seemed the loss of my mother had Glennis thinking anew. Wasn't I suffering enough?

I cleaned up my hand and put a bandage around it and I served breakfast. No one even looked at me as I did so, not even my father. He didn't enquire how I was doing after finding out about my mother's death. Instead, he was discussing decorating the living room with my stepmother and telling her it wasn't necessary. Great. The tautness of her jaw showed me I'd probably suffer for him saying no to her later.

Hanging around, I waited until he was about to leave. My stepmother kissed him goodbye and left and just before he pulled the front door closed, I leaped out and opened it back up. He startled.

"Ella, really. Is one dead parent not enough for you, that you want to frighten me to death too?"

"How did she die?" I asked him.

He looked at his watch. "A brain aneurism they believe, though it has to be confirmed by a coroner. Mr Salinger said she'd had headaches infrequently, but that afternoon she just clutched her head then fell down immediately dead. He said there was nothing he could do."

"And what about her funeral arrangements?"

He shook his head as if bewildered by my words. "How should I know? It doesn't concern me, does it? Now, excuse me, Ella, I need to get to work, and so do you."

He headed towards the driver who was holding open the passenger door for him.

I dropped down onto the top step and put my head in my hands. Dad wasn't interested in the funeral of my mum and so it was possibly a pauper's grave for her and no one there to mourn. No way for me to say goodbye.

"Mother, quickly, Ella is sat outside the house making a complete show of herself," Jemima shouted. I got up and pushed past her, running back down to the cellar where I locked myself in and threw myself down on the bed. And then the storm cloud grew ever angrier within me at what life had served me so far. Somehow, I needed to get to that castle once I was eighteen. I needed to ask the man there about my mother. To beg for his help with burying her properly.

Once I knew I was alone in the house, I emerged and set to my tasks. Someone had smeared jam all over the dining room. It was on the table legs, the walls, and the broken jar smashed into many pieces and all over the rug. They thought they could break me, but instead it occupied my mind, and stopped me from dwelling on the things I couldn't change right now. My hand throbbed all day though as I worked through the chores, and when I stood at the medicine cabinet, for a brief moment I thought about emptying medicines into all of their drinks and being done with the lot of them. I settled for two paracetamol for myself, and a hope that karma would deal with things.

For a brief moment in time some days, I had time spare and was alone, and when this happened, I would put music on and pretend I lived the life of a poet or dreamer. I'd dance around the room as if I were wearing an ethereal dress with lace and gossamer and imagine picnics with a beloved, sat by a lake, looking out as the sun lit up the water and dazzled my eyes. My grey self would wonder upon the different coloured blooms around us and slowly, my lover would bring out his artist's palette and paint me by numbers back to life.

I never saw the face of this lover, and I imagined maybe I never would. That it might not be in my future to be anything but dull and muted. My hand in marriage offered by my father to some old cruel bastard in return for a share in an emerging business. My having to serve not only in the household but in the bedroom too, having to pretend the wrinkling aging flesh were something wonderful.

I went into the dustbin and ferreted around the bottom for the pieces of broken plate and then returning to my room I threw them with venom at my walls over and over, and hit them with an old, displaced brick until they were nothing but slivers and dust, impossible to ever piece together again. I ran my hand through the mess, uncaring as to whether any sharp remnants might tear into my skin. I smiled. Tomorrow, I would place some of the dust into my stepmother's breakfast. Just a speck that would go unnoticed. I would grind up every bit of the plate and feed it to her until either the plate had gone, or I had. She had said it was her favourite after all.

While eating their evening meal, I heard my mother's name mentioned. I'd been about to collect the empty soup bowls, but I hovered near the doorway instead.

"This is the strangest thing I ever heard, Grant. Who throws a ball after a funeral?"

My ears pricked up.

"Salinger apparently. He said that Freya had served him extremely well over the years and so not only would he ensure she was buried in the grounds of Moonstone Castle in the absence of any family to take care of things, but he would arrange this ball afterward."

"For whom though? Freya had no one but Ella," Glennis asked, clearly agitated.

"For us, for Ella, and for some selected other guests who he'd been meaning to catch up with and hadn't, he said. It did sound very strange, but then by all accounts he's a strange man. Anyway, we can always say no."

"But I want to go and see the castle, Mum," Danica whined. "I mean, how old is this man? He lives alone, right? We could get to know him better, and then, who knows, he might bequeath us the building."

"Ooh, yes, mother. Please could we go, Father? Just for a little while," Jemima pleaded.

I felt the pain that always speared my heart when either of my two stepsisters called him father or dad. But then he was that to them, had been for years now.

"What would you like to do, Glennis?" he asked.

"I think we should go, but not Ella. We'll say she's ill. What date is this ball anyway?"

"This Saturday, December 18th. Burial at seven thirty, ball eight pm until midnight."

It was the day before my birthday. Mr Salinger was burying my mother and they weren't going to let me go. Then his ball would end as my eighteenth began.

Maybe I could run while they were out?

Take as much from the house as I could and escape?

"I can't believe I've got to stand at the grave of your ex-wife and pretend to grieve for her," Glennis huffed. "But I'll do it for my daughters. For Danica and Jemima, who might enchant the mysterious Mr Salinger."

"I'll let him know," my father said, and at that point I knocked and entered the room to clear away the dishes.

I didn't miss the smug look my stepsisters gave me and the sly one from my stepmother.

"We'll all be out on Saturday evening, Ella, so we won't require dinner that evening," Glennis informed me.

"Yes, Stepmother," I replied.

"Now I think we shall probably all have new outfits for the occasion, but just in case, I shall pick out a few reserve outfits and you can make any necessary alterations and updates," she declared. "You can come to our rooms and stand there while we decide."

And that's what I did. I stood and watched while all their designer clothes, shoes, and accessories were paraded in front of me, and they all delighted in doing so. Then they sent me away with piles of clothes that they said needed altering: a higher hem here and a shorter sleeve there. Yet I knew they'd never wear them because of course they would buy brand new.

I might just set the lot alight at midnight as an early birthday present to myself.

There were five days to freedom.

Five days to suffer these fools.

Until the clock struck midnight...

CHAPTER 5

ELLA

The days passed as all those before them had. If there was a difference, I thought I caught excited chatter from my stepsisters, but their voices quieted whenever I came near, so I couldn't be sure if this was real or just my imagination from being left out of things.

I satisfied myself by continuing to feed my stepmother her broken plate, and by plotting my escape.

Before I knew it, Saturday was upon us.

My family stood at the front door ready to depart. Where I would usually be in the cellar by now, I appeared and took in their brand-new black attire. Dark suit for my father, dark dresses with jackets for the women.

'Is your dinner at a wake?" I enquired brazenly, knowing I wouldn't suffer for it later because I wouldn't be here.

"Yes, it's to mark the death of your personality," Jemima retorted, and Danica sniggered.

"The dress code for the evening's soiree is black and elegant. Not that you'd know anything about elegance," Glennis scoffed.

"I mean when was the last time you even bathed?" Danica made a retching noise.

"Other than my evening chores, is there anything else?" I queried my stepmother before landing my eyes on my father, who'd said nothing so far and who had been staring at his phone throughout the exchange.

"We're going to be late," he said, not even looking at me, and he opened the door. They all turned towards the doorway and began to file out.

My stepmother was the last to leave and before she closed the door she said, "There is a birthday present for you in the living room."

And then it was just me. Seven pm and home alone. I went in search of the 'present' which I felt sure would be more crushed jam in a rug.

To my surprise, in the living room was a scarlet red box with a gold ribbon wrapped around with an elaborate bow. Had my father made her get me a gift?

I dropped to my knees in front of the box and pulled open the ribbon and then I cast off the lid. Inside was a mass of circles of emerald-green confetti. I plunged my hand inside to see what else was in there, only to find my own watch, the face cracked and broken. And then I realised... the green 'confetti' was made from my mother's dress. Glennis had obliterated my final two possessions of my mother.

I felt my shoulders drag low as they lost their tension, defeat heavy in my body. She'd taken everything from me: my father, my home, my pride, my final links to my mother. In that box was indeed her 'gift', her birthday message that now things would be even worse.

But if I had only one treasured item, she and my stepsisters held onto many possessions to show their wealth. *I will destroy everything*, I ranted inwardly as I got back to my feet. My body trembled with anger as it roiled inside me, and I raced upstairs as it tore through me.

But every room was locked. All with shiny and new mechanisms. I could not get into a single one of them. In fact, as I retraced my steps and returned downstairs, the only room I could get into apart from the cellar was the living room. The room she'd wanted to decorate, and my father had told her was perfectly fine. She was deliberately baiting me. She wanted me to ruin it. That was her goal. Then I was the villain of the piece, and she got what she wanted. *Again.*

Carrying the box containing the circles of cloth, I returned to the cellar. I pulled out my sewing kit and got to work. I had time before I left for the castle.

I pulled the threadbare sheet off my mattress and stripped out of my grey jogging suit. Wrapping the sheet around myself, I marked with a pen where to cut, and fashioned an extremely rough dress. A tube top with unhemmed straps, an A-line skirt that tied around me. There was nothing sophisticated about it. But I glued on circle after circle, and stitched the holes where I could, until the material became covered in green. I had no idea what it looked like on, and I could bet it was a monstrosity, but I was wearing my mother's dress. Fixing my broken watch in place, I thanked God that my computer still held the time. I had no doubt this would be going next. I presumed the only reason it remained now was that it would have easily tipped me off to the fact Glennis had been in here.

I was done. I would go visit my mother at her grave dressed in her gown and then I would beg the owner to grant me the safety of his castle.

But why would he do that, Ella?

Why would he bring trouble to his own door?

Maybe I wouldn't ask him after all. Perhaps after I'd said my final goodbyes to my mum, I would run away somewhere no one knew me and start over.

I decided I would not dwell on anything else right now other than to go to my mum's grave. Going to the battered hamper I kept my clothes in, I found it empty of anything but my tattered jogging suits. She'd taken my coat and shoes.

There was nothing else for it. I wrapped my feet in more of the remaining bedsheet and I went up to the hallway and left by the back door... Where I came face to face with a small woman with spiky black hair with orange tips. She took one look at me and tutted.

"Oh my dear, that will not do at all. Not for the ball."

I lowered my head to stare at her, feeling my face flush as she stared back at me, assessing every part of me.

"I suppose my stepmother sent you to ensure I didn't leave the house?" I snarked.

"Incorrect. Mr Salinger sent me to make sure you did leave the house. He promised your mother that he would bring you to her on your eighteenth birthday and though we're a little early so far, we do have things to do. So, first things first, whatever I do for you, do not thank me. I do this at Mr Salinger's request, but I am fae. If I receive your thanks, you will owe me a debt. I've told you now, so it's on you if you don't listen."

"Fae?"

"Yes, I'm from the realm of faerie, but I really don't think now is the time to address the validity of my statement. It shall delay us. Let's move first, ask questions later. Now." She looked at me. "I know you've made a significant effort with your attire, but if you'll just allow me." She waved a finger at me and the 'dress' I was wearing rippled and turned into a deep green. So dark it almost looked black. It was silk. Square necked and capped sleeved, it fit my upper body and then flowed out slightly. Enough to move in. Her finger touched my wrist and my watch repaired and began to tick. Next, the fae's finger went to my head, and I felt my hair wrap itself up in a plait down my back. My skin felt different, and I touched my lip to find a crimson stain painted on it.

The finger twirled again, and boots appeared on my feet. Heeled and yet they felt like downy pillows were wrapped around them.

She sucked on her lip. "You need a bag too. Now just know that none of this is real. It's a glamour I'm placing on you, and it will disappear at midnight at your mother's grave. You will now go to the ball where your family will not be aware that it is you. So let all your pent-up anxiety leave you now. You will go to the ball, and you will pay your respects to your mother. Mr Salinger will explain all. Your mother spoke of you so much. He would like the opportunity to catch up with you."

I nodded. My brain was still trying to catch up with what was happening right now. If I woke later and found Glennis had drugged me, I shouldn't be surprised, but while the trip (meant figuratively and literally) was happening, I was going to enjoy it regardless.

"Okay. Now let's get out onto the street. Your carriage awaits," she said. I followed her and found a black limousine idling at the kerb, its windows tinted. The door opened on its own and the fae woman who herself was dressed in a black lace dress and laced up heeled boots jumped in first. She patted the seat beside her, and I climbed in too.

There was a privacy screen up preventing me from seeing the driver, but all I was interested in was staring out of the windows. In six years, I had been no further than the park. Now my eyes took in my surroundings as we made our way up to Moonstone Castle.

"I'm sorry. I never asked you your name," I said to the fae beside me, though I never took my eyes from the view.

"My name is Iris, but you need not apologise. I should imagine your mind is overrun with questions, mainly wondering whether this is real."

"I don't care if it's real or not. I'm going to my mother's grave to pay my respects and that's enough for me right now. Whatever this is, I hope I get there."

"You will get there, because this *is* real."

I turned to her then. "But even a dream person could give me that answer, couldn't they?"

She chuckled and I turned back to the window.

The car left the village and went onto wider roads before country lanes appeared. The driver paused near a pair of massive ornate gates, and I heard the creak as they opened. It was dark as we made our way up the winding road, I presumed towards the castle. The trees canopied over the uneven road, and I pictured my mum having made her way here, awed at the fact she'd walked all the way to Mr Salinger's door.

And then Moonstone Castle came into view. There was lighting around it and the building was lit from within, but the moon shone off the white stone, causing the castle to appear in the spotlight of its brilliance. I gasped at its beauty. We pulled up outside the front entrance and my door opened again, but this time a small, dark-haired fellow was at the other side.

I turned back to Iris. "Fae?"

"There are many fae here tonight."

"Right, looks like I'll be forgetting my manners then. In other words, I'll act like my family."

Iris laughed.

The fae helped me out of the car and directed me inside. "Iris will accompany you to meet Mr Salinger and the other guests in the banqueting hall," he said.

A banqueting hall. Who had such things in this day and age? I bet my stepmother and stepsisters were green with envy and sucking up a storm around Mr Salinger.

We followed the sound of music until we came outside of a large doorway. Inside, I could see an enormous table with more fae milling around it, and then as I stepped into the room, at the other end was a dance floor where my family were dancing.

Only my family.

But I didn't have chance to consider the strangeness of the looks of utter joy on their faces as I was disturbed by Iris shaking my arm. "Ella, Mr Salinger would like to introduce himself."

"Oh, okay," I said, turning around to meet the host.

My mouth dropped open as I came face to face with the strange man from the park.

CHAPTER 6

BEAU

"You," she said, her eyes first widening and then narrowing as various emotions flickered across her features.

"My name is Beau. Beau Salinger." I bowed to her. "It's a pleasure to have you here, Ella."

Her head shot over to her family. "Don't say my name."

I laughed in deep amusement and threaded my arm through hers. "Come, let me show you how you can enjoy your evening without having to worry about your family."

Her body stiffened with its proximity to mine, but then she steeled herself. "God, you're so bloody cold. Perhaps you need a smaller house that you can afford to heat."

"Oh, Ella, always so charming."

"Iris told me I have a glamour. I know they won't recognise me. You don't need to drag me over to them, I'd rather stay over here."

I smiled at her. "Ella, for once, quit arguing with me. I promise you it'll be worth it."

Huffing, she let me escort her over to her family.

I stopped in front of them and let go of Ella's arm. "Call them. Any one of them," I instructed.

After first rolling her eyes she shouted, "Dad?"

He stopped, turned towards her, and said, "Won't you come dance? It's so much fun!" Then he turned back and carried on.

"So you've got them drunk then," she stated.

"Nope. Much, much better than drunk."

"Drugged?"

"Nope."

"Mr Salinger, just get to the point. They're acting very strangely, and they all look... oh hypnotised. You've had them hypnotised."

"In a fashion."

She smiled herself then. "Does that mean you can get them to do anything?"

"Not at the moment. All they can do right now is dance. But I could make them do anything if they weren't spelled by the fae."

"Gosh, the fae are busy this evening. Glamours, hypnotising people to dance. Whatever next?"

"That's up to you," I said. "Only I know how they've treated you, Ella, and I think it's time you had a little revenge."

Her posture stiffened again. "What do you mean, you know how they've treated me?"

I softened my tone. "I've watched you, Ella. Watched and kept your secrets. Told your mother you were well so she wouldn't worry. But I know about the cellar, about you being their servant."

"But my mother didn't find out?" Her voice wobbled a little.

"No, and should she have survived, I was bringing you here to her on your eighteenth. But more on that later. I'm so sorry about your mum, but right now, I'm more interested in dealing with these fools. They chose to dance to fae music and now they are entranced. Unless you break them out of it, they will dance until they die."

She studied them some more, tilting her head as she did so. She pulled in, then slowly released a deep breath. I found it enchanting given I no longer had need of my own.

"Penny for your thoughts?"

"You'll have to excuse me. I'm not sure what to think."

I huff-laughed. "Oh, Ella, that's not true, is it? You've thought plenty since you've stood there. About how you hope their feet are bleeding and that they're in pain. The answer is they haven't been dancing enough yet, but they will be getting tired. And you've also pictured every one of them dead. Especially your stepmother. You even thought of standing over her and laughing."

"What are you?" she demanded.

"I'm a vampire."

She took several steps back from me. "Don't be ridiculous."

"Ah, the denial. There can't possibly be fae, or vampires, just sad little humans." I let my fangs descend and my eyes go red. "Why do you think I live up here all alone?"

She stared at me. "Suppose I believe you? Vampires can hypnotize, can they not? Put thoughts in people's heads. Maybe you suggested to my mother that she was all alone with you, but you had a castle full of staff and company. You'd better have not taken advantage of her."

I loved that faced with a vampire, or the possibility of one, Ella was still spitting her venom.

"I cared deeply for your mother in a platonic way. She became a dear friend. Why do you think I'm going to all this trouble to bring you here and to deal with these... lesser individuals?"

"That's why you're so cold," she said, so quietly I wondered if it was meant only for her own ears.

I raised a brow. "You believe me?"

She scoffed. "I told myself I would continue on with this strange evening without questioning if I'm insane or not. I can choose to debate with you, or I can enjoy seeing my family suffer and then go to my mother's grave."

"I applaud your choice. Now, what do you wish to happen to your family?"

"For now, I wish for them to continue dancing. Until their feet are bleeding at the very least."

I whooped. "Excellent." I turned to the other fae. "Ella has said for the dance to continue. Enjoy all." With that instruction, most of the fae joined in, spinning her family around and around, tormenting them as they were trapped with insane grinning expressions and bodies that wouldn't stop moving, while their minds suffered with a slow onslaught of madness.

I offered my crooked elbow to her. "Shall we somewhere quieter to talk before I take you to your mother? I promised it would be on your eighteenth birthday, and so I'm sorry but we have a couple of hours to pass yet this evening." I saw her eye the food. "Faerie food," I explained. "Eat that and you will belong to the fae realm. I will fix you something myself from the kitchen, though it won't be much."

Ella took my arm, and we walked out of the room.

The kitchen was only a short distance away, given it needed to be near to the banqueting hall. I watched as Ella looked around the hallway as we walked together.

"Was my mum happy here, or did she lie to me, as I lied to her?"

"Your mother was very content here. I will show you her rooms. She spent a lot of time sewing and doing other crafts. I kept different hours to your mum, but she would always make sure to stay up to see me. In fact, quite often she would also turn night into day so we could converse." I tapped her arm. "If she could have afforded it, she would have fought to the death to get you back, Ella, and if I had had wealth at my disposal, I would have helped her."

"Why? Because you became friends?"

"Yes, and because her love for you shone out of her like the moonlight shines on my castle. Strong and dimmed only when challenged by other factors. I offered to kill them, but she wouldn't let me. She thought you were getting an education."

"Oh, I was. At first. My father believed in training from the ground up. Unfortunately, he forgot he'd put me there. This flower didn't get the chance to bloom."

I stared into her eyes. "I beg to differ, *bella*. I think the very fact you bloomed regardless is why your step-family kept you in the dark. But they didn't take into account the fact that seeds need darkness to germinate."

She rubbed the back of her neck, her discomfort at my appraisal showing, but we'd reached the kitchen now, so I requested she follow me. Opening up the fridge, I found nothing edible remaining. The pantry revealed a jar of pasta sauce and an unopened packet of pasta. My face must have given away my discomfort, because she took them from my hands.

"Honestly, I'm invited to a ball and the human is not catered for."

"I forgot. I apologise."

"I already ate to be honest," she said, putting the items back. "I'd have eaten a slice of cake, or a bun, but I think for now, I'll make myself a black coffee and be satisfied with that." She put the pasta and sauce away, and searched out a mug, before spooning coffee from the cannister into it. She then filled the kettle and switched it on.

"Why aren't you afraid of me?" I enquired.

She shrugged. "If you plan to harm me, there's nothing I can do about it. Plus, I might be hallucinating or tripping. I can't be bothered to do anything but focus on seeing my mother's grave right now."

She finished making the drink and then sat at the dining table. "So how do I stop you reading my mind?" she asked.

"Spoilsport," I replied, but I taught her anyway.

I was delighted at what a quick learner she was and how enthusiastic her questions were about my species and that of the fae.

We'd been talking for ages, but her eyes kept looking at her watch.

"It's a quarter to midnight. At what time should we leave?"

"In another five minutes. Your mother is not far away," I said.

She nodded. "At midnight I lose my beautiful gown."

I shrugged. "It is a false glamour anyway. But after,

I will take you to your mother's rooms and show you that you have other things to wear."

"She left me clothes?"

"She *made* you clothes. She asked you how much you'd grown, and she worked out your sizes. She made so much that some things must fit."

Ella bit her lip hard.

"You can show emotion, Ella."

"I will. But I'm saving it for the one person who deserves it," she answered.

———————

At ten minutes to the hour, we rose and left the room and walked a short distance to an outer door. Pushing through, we traversed a gravelled path until we approached the point where it crossed through a large hedge. Continuing on and turning left was the newly filled in grave of Freya Story.

"I'll let you choose a headstone to mark the grave and you may visit whenever, and plant whatever you like around the space," I told her.

"Did my father and stepfamily attend the burial?" she asked.

"No. That was a ruse. I've had them dancing since

they arrived. Only I, Iris, and a priest buried your mother."

"Thank you for being there for her and allowing me to visit."

Footsteps sounded out behind us, and Iris appeared.

"There's one minute to go."

We stood silent together, waiting.

"Five... four... three... two... one."

Ella's glamour disappeared and I saw her again as she'd been in the park. Ethereally beautiful, her blonde hair now loose. She was dressed in a strange costume that appeared home-made by someone blind drunk. She looked down at herself and back at me. "I'll explain later."

Walking over to her mother's grave, she knelt down at the foot of it. Placing a hand in the small patch of soil left at the side, she picked up a handful and let it fall on the mound of earth.

A greying arm shot through the soil reaching for her, its fingernails packed with dirt, and she screamed.

"Don't be afraid, Ella," Iris spoke softly. "Take your mother's hand and say goodbye properly. We're in the witching hour and this is the only time you'll have with her."

"I... I can see my mother? Say goodbye?" she stuttered as she checked with Iris.

"Yes, sweetheart. You can."

"Th- great. I mean great," she uttered through eyes awash with unshed tears.

And then she leaned over and grasped the hand of her deceased mother and disappeared from our view into the realm of the in-between.

Chapter 7

Ella

My mother appeared in front of me, as solid as if she were alive. Her body wasn't in any state of decay. She looked well. At peace. She threw her arms open, and I stepped within them, as my senses tried to process everything.

A new grave, a decaying hand, a shimmer in the air, and then here I was, in a place of just blackness, a void. Except me and my mother were held within it.

For a moment it was disorientating. My feet held as if there were ground beneath them, and yet I could see nothing apart from my mum.

"Ella," she said as she stroked my hair. "I'm so very sorry I didn't come for you."

I pulled back. "Don't be, Mum. I know you did everything you could. D-did you suffer?" I asked.

"When I died?"

I nodded.

"No, it was quick. So quick that I know my place on earth was meant to be only that short stint. I wholly believe I was there just to birth you, Ella, so you could step into the life that will light you up. After the rain comes rainbows, they say, after all."

She moved her hand and two chairs appeared. "Shall we sit and chat, because we don't have much time?"

I nodded again. It seemed words were hard to come by for the moment. Faced with one final hour with my mother, how did I make the most of it? I would never see her again. Staring at her, I tried to commit every cell of her body to memory.

She shook her head. "It will all fade anyway, Ella. It helps us move on."

"I will not forget you, Mum."

"I know, honey. Nor I you. You were my greatest achievement, Ella."

Emotion choked my throat, and a tear ran down my cheek. Reaching over, she wiped it away. "You are so beautiful."

"I got it from my mum," I told her, and we both laughed.

"So what's on the other side?" I asked her.

"I can't tell you. That's why we have the in-between. No one is allowed over until it is their time, and I hope yours will be far away."

"I'm not sure what to do now," I confessed honestly. "My father and his family are trapped in a fae dance, and I need to decide what to do now I'm eighteen. Where I'm going. What were your plans for us?"

"For us to continue at the castle for the moment. I didn't think beyond us being reunited because your future was for you to choose, not me."

I sighed. "Did Mr Salinger treat you right?"

"Beau became a dear friend."

"But no romance?" I clarified.

"God, no. Not my type at all." She laughed. "I prefer a muscled blonde, not that I ever bothered trying to meet anyone after your father. But Beau is a good man. Guarded though. I spent a lot of time with him, but don't feel I ever got beyond the surface of him."

I thought of the man who'd had me brought to my mum. Who'd watched over me for years. Who'd began punishing my father and stepfamily. Who'd arranged for me to see my mum one final time. Why? Because he respected my mum and had forged this friendship with her? Was that all? Or was there something else? Had our situation triggered something within him? Helping to heal an old wound of his own?

And why was I relieved there'd been nothing between him and my mum?

———

Mum chatted and told me of her years at the castle. How she'd prepared for my arrival and hoped I'd consider staying there.

"Beau will be in dire need of a housekeeper again. And he can't continue with selling pieces from the house. He needs a way forward, Ella. You might be exactly what he needs. Talk to him when you return. Ask if you can stay—at least until you figure out your next move."

I wondered if that would be agreeable to him. That I take hold of the reins dropped by my mum. The castle was beautiful, and I'd love to explore the grounds.

"I will. I think I'd like to stay, for a while at least. To be where you were and follow in your footsteps."

"No, Ella. Make your own footprints at Moonstone Castle."

An impression of my family dancing came to me. "Is it bad that I'm taking delight in the fact Dad and the rest of them are suffering trapped in the dance? I know I should let them go, be better than them, but they deserve what they've got."

She patted my arm. "I wish I had known the truth before I passed over. Maybe I would have sent Beau to deal with them."

"We can't change what happened, Mum. But I guess I have to be the better person and let them go, right?"

"Embrace who you are, Ella, and do what feels right. That's all I can advise you."

The image of her glitched.

"What's happening?"

"I'm being called back. Our time is almost done." She stood up. "Let me hold you again, my daughter, for one last time."

We placed our arms around one another, and she stroked my hair. As she kissed the top of my head, I felt everything tear from around me, and found myself knelt back at the graveside.

A scream tore through me at being apart from my mum, knowing I'd never see her again. Then a tall, cold man pulled me to my feet and put his arms around me, holding me tight, as I sagged against him and cried.

"Let's get you back inside," Beau said.

I nodded and let him lead me back into the castle. Right now, I couldn't look at my mum's grave again. I would; I'd probably return and chat to her at her grave-side many times. Even though she'd never reply again. But right now, my emotions were raw, and I was strangely finding comfort and support from the weird man I barely knew.

"Would you like to go see her suite of rooms or is that too much for today?" he asked.

"Too much, for now. Do you have a room where I could sit for a while and just gather myself a little?"

"Sure," he said.

We finally entered a large formal sitting room. I flopped down on the sofa and Beau went to a cabinet where he poured us both a drink.

He walked over and handed mine to me.

"What is it?"

"Port."

I sniffed it. "I've never drunk alcohol before."

"It will take the edge off, that's all. You've had a shock. I still think Iris should have forewarned you, but she said you were better to not have time to think on it."

There were so many questions in my head: about my mother, the paranormal, but I was quite simply depleted. I took small sip of the port. It was warming, soothing.

"The first time I spoke to your mother she sat right where you are," he said.

"Mr Salinger."

"Beau. You must call me Beau."

"Beau. Would it be okay if I stayed for the evening?"

"Of course. It's okay with me if you wish to stay forever, Ella."

I tilted my head. "That is a peculiar thing to say to someone you barely know. However, I'm too tired to query it tonight."

I finished the drink, feeling my eyes drooping and before I knew it, the world blinked out.

My eyes fluttered open and took in a painted ceiling, with ornamental coving that was broken off in places. *The castle*, I remembered, sitting up. A large blanket fell off my shoulders. Beau was reading, sitting in the armchair to the side of me. It was still dark.

"What time is it?"

"Three thirty. I will be off to my own bedroom

shortly. But before I go, there is the small matter of your family to deal with."

That woke me up. "Are they *still* dancing?"

"Of course. Until you say otherwise."

I threw the blanket to one side. "Come on. Take me back to the banqueting hall."

I rubbed at my eyes and tried to wake up. My body argued that it still needed the rest of its sleep, but I pressed on regardless. We reached the hall and sure enough, the music still played, and my family still danced. But now the agony upon their features was tenfold what it had been before. Rictus grins that belonged in horror movies.

"If we stop the dance, what else is in your repertoire to deal with them?" I asked Beau.

"Drained, either quickly or super slowly. I do prefer a slow torture personally. Or I can do the simple thing of removing you from their lives by the power of suggestion."

"You can just make them forget I existed with your compulsion?"

He sighed. "You're going to pick that option, aren't you, and here I was thinking you might like to play on the dark side. How disappointing."

His words reminded me that he was a vampire, a bloodsucker, a killer. But I wasn't and he had to accept that. "The power of suggestion it is," I said. "However, no one said we couldn't have some fun with it."

My words seemed to appease him, and he smirked. "Do go on."

———

Beau got Iris to stop the dance, and the fae bid us goodnight. I stood in the hall with Beau as my family came back to the land of the living.

They all promptly fell to their knees. My father clutched his heart. "What on earth is happening? I think I may die."

My stepmother looked at me. Even exhausted she managed to say, "What is she doing here? And what the hell is she wearing?"

My sisters were looking at their now bare feet, which were bleeding, blistered, and sore, as if they'd spent hours wearing shoes that didn't fit.

I realised my own feet now had the most beautiful ballet slippers on them. Beau must have done this while I was asleep. I wondered if they'd been my mother's. Whoever's they were they fit perfectly.

My sisters began to weep. "Mother, the pain," Danica cried.

"Mr Salinger," Glennis said. "What happened? Is it

the food? We all seem a little the worse for wear." She clutched her head then. "I don't feel at all well."

"Let me answer your first question. What is Ella doing here? She's here because tonight was the funeral of her dear mother. Now you informed me that she was ill with a headache and yet when my friend went to the house, she discovered that Ella was in fact perfectly fine. So I had her brought here as per my original invitation."

Glennis began to say something, but then turned a shade of green and put a hand over her mouth.

"I don't wish to hear anything else from you anyway," Beau said. He bent down and looked into her eyes. "From now on you have lost the ability to say a word," he said. Her pupils seemed to dilate and then she blinked and sat silent.

"I demand you call transport for us and allow us to return home," my father snarled. "Ella, don't just stand there. Help us for goodness' sake."

"I fully intend to, Father," I replied, and he nodded satisfied. I knelt down nearer to him. "Remember when you told me I needed to learn about not having money? From the ground up, you said? Well, it seems to me like not only did you forget all about me, *Daddy*, while I became your servant and not your daughter, but you forgot about your own spiel. So,

Beau and I are going to make sure you do remember. You're going to give away all your wealth and have to start again."

My father scoffed. "As if I'd do that. Honestly, have you taken leave of your senses? I should have known. Your maternal grandmother wasn't of sound mind. It's clearly gone down the DNA. I did not forget you were my daughter, Ella. I just decided I didn't want you anymore. You reminded me of your mum too much."

I gasped, but he wasn't done.

"Even though you look different, you were always just so close. I could hardly bear to look at you. You have Glennis to thank for keeping you with us at all."

"As a maid?" I scoffed.

He shrugged.

"I've changed my mind. Drain him," I ordered Beau while I kept my gaze on my father. I saw the flicker of fear in his gaze and it made me my stomach flip with anticipation and need.

"Drain? What do you mean, Ella?" my father asked. "What are you talking about?" "Oh I get it. Like rinse me, take all my money. I heard you were broke," he addressed Beau with distaste. "I'm sure we can come to some agreement if you can just get us that taxi."

• • •

I clicked my fingers in front of my father's face to get his attention back on me. "I mean for every bit of your blood to slowly leave your body. The pain so intense you may pass out, though I hope you do not. I hope you feel every bit of suffering and yet I can tell you it will be nothing at the side of what you put me through for all these years."

I turned my back on him and turned to Beau. "Do it."

"Are you sure, Ella?" Beau checked.

"Never been surer in my life and I'm going to watch every minute. Freeze the others in place and mute my sisters' mouths too," I ordered.

Hate burned in my veins. A strong need within me to feed off their distress.

"Your wish is my command," Beau answered.

CHAPTER 8

BEAU

Her taste for vengeance was an elixir to my damned soul. I could hear the quickening of Ella's heartbeat and the rush of blood through her veins.

I moved forward, flexing and unflexing my fingers, observing my targets and biding my time.

I let my fangs descend and I now saw the world through a red haze. The women's eyes all widened, and the girls were about to scream, so I suggested they stopped like their mother. I froze them all in place, to be dealt with one by one. Starting with Grant Story.

Hunger and need coursed through me because I could smell Ella's taste for revenge and her blood sang to me like a bespoke blend, as her darker side emerged.

I stared into Grant's eyes. "Come to me," I

commanded.

His skin mottled with his anger and frustration that despite his unwillingness he moved towards me, and every step was a pained one due to his sore feet.

He turned to Ella. "Please, Ella, save me. I know now I did wrong by you. It was her fault." He pointed at Glennis. "She seduced me and blackmailed me."

Ella wandered closer to him. "Oh, poor, sweet Daddy. Were you corrupted by the widow with two daughters? Did her vagina sing you some kind of hypnotic song? Entrance you like a snake out of a basket?" He made a grab for her arm. She looked down at it, looked up at him and scoffed.

"You let me live in the cellar and forgot I was your daughter. You said yourself you didn't want me. I received not one word of consolation at the loss of my mother. Wasn't brought here to bury her, and now you want me, or rather my help?" She spat in his face. "Kill him," she demanded, before she went to stand near her stepfamily. "Keep their bodies unable to move a step, but their brains and expressions in perfect working order," she requested.

I froze Grant's feet to the floor before I spoke to the rest of them with the suggestion.

And then I moved back swiftly and told Grant, "You'll feel everything," before I ripped into his neck.

I fed greedily. The man may have been an imbecile, but he was still food, and in life he'd eaten well. It meant his blood was satisfying. My eyes fixed on Ella's as I drained him. Her own watched in fascination. There was no horror on her face, no regret. Just a pleased expression. I threw Grant's empty corpse to the floor like the trash it was.

Then I waited, because I was standing there with blood dripping from my mouth, and my clothes were soaked with more. Soon the reality would set in, and Ella would run. The thoughts of what a vampire did were very different to the visual of what a vampire did.

Ella turned to her stepmother. "You're next," she said, and she laughed. Glennis' mouth was wide in silent shock. Her protests lost. "Have you been feeling precious this week?" Ella asked her. "Only you know the plate that broke, the one you stabbed me with? I ground it up and fed it to you." She leaned in closer. "You wasted six years of my life and in return you're going to lose the rest of yours."

She looked at me. "Take my father's body back to the house and get Glennis to confess to killing him. I don't care that there'll be a mystery of how she managed to drain all his blood. And then these two..." she eyed her two sisters. "I think they want cake. What will happen to them if they go to faerie?"

"They'll be the servants of the royals."

"Perfection." Ella walked over to the table and got a selection of buns and cakes.

"I'll be back shortly. In the meantime. Girls, you are very hungry," I said.

My strength meant carrying Grant's dead body and Glennis' alive one was nothing. By the time I put them back in Ella's former home, Glennis was covered in Grant's blood. I called the police and stayed long enough to suggest to them that this case was cut and dried, and the result of an argument where all three sisters had left home because Grant was abusive to them.

When I returned, Ella was sitting with an empty plate and her sisters appeared inebriated. Six of the fae sat with them.

"All sorted?" she asked.

"All the I's dotted and T's crossed."

"The fae are here to take Jemima and Danica. I just asked them to hold on for in case you needed to give them any instructions I wasn't aware of."

"They're for the worst of the fae," I said. "Enjoy them."

The fae nodded and their hands grabbed greedily at the sisters as I freed them from my powers of suggestion.

We heard their garbled screams and then they were gone.

"Come," I held out a hand to Ella. "You can sleep in one of the rooms I have for you upstairs. I must go to bed now before the dawn rises.

And then it came. Reality.

Ella's body began to shake uncontrollably. "W-what's happening to me?"

"It's the adrenaline," I explained. "Focus on your breathing. It will pass."

"Is he really dead?" she asked.

I arched a brow. "It's too late for regret, Ella."

She shook her head. "No, not regret, just... he can't come back?"

"No. A change can only occur if the blood is swapped. He would have had to drink my blood in return. He is gone, and so are the rest of your family. You can feel guilty for the rest of your life about it if you choose, but you can change none of it now."

"I feel numb."

'It's the shock.'

"I want to f-feel something," she said, her eyes on mine, doe-like.

And then she closed the space between us, coming up on tiptoes, her lips on mine, kissing me. I kissed her back hungrily, feeling the thirst in me awaken, but not for her blood. I was hungry for her body.

Then I caught the glimmer of dawn break through the window, the shine of it on the corner of the floor.

Breaking off our connection, I noted the blood of her father smeared across her mouth.

"I have to go," I said. "I'll be back when it's dark." I departed the room for my sanctuary and wondered if she'd still be there when I returned.

In my room I paced the floor thinking of what I'd shown Ella on her first visit. I'd promised her mother that I'd bring her to her and had done so by bringing her to her mother's graveside. I'd not promised to murder her father. Not promised to let her kiss me.

But I couldn't deny my attraction to her. It felt like she was my missing breath. The moment I'd spoken to Ella in the park I'd been enraptured and then tonight... she'd been a delightful surprise: magnificent, powerful... unexpectedly and majestically malicious. Vampires walked both sides. Thought to be murderous, we were maligned. But we could be lit by the light of the moon and be good people too. Balance was the right recipe of life, was it not?

I wondered what Ella was doing now. What she was thinking. Whether she had in fact run. But I knew even if she had, I would go and try to find her. She was under my skin. I'd had what a normal man would see as one simple taste. A quick but passionate kiss. But I was a vampire. Her kiss danced on my tongue, beyond the water of her saliva—electrolytes, enzymes, proteins, etc. The scent of her arousal hit my nostrils like a runaway train. Her quickened breath and heartbeat the train's motion on the track. It had hit me with no means of escape, even if I'd wanted to. My cock was hard in my pants, my fangs descended with lust. I was fully fed and content in appetite and yet still hungry.

For Ella's sweet, chaste desire. I knew no man had been near her. She was pure, untouched by anything except for maybe her own hands.

I craved her, felt pangs where my heart resided but didn't beat.

I yawned then as tiredness hit. The dawn had no doubt fully broken now. My eyes felt heavy. Ensuring the wards on my room were in place, I crawled into my bed and closed my eyes.

But for the first time in years, I couldn't wait to be awake again.

CHAPTER 9

ELLA

He was gone. I sank back to my knees on the dance floor and looked around me. The shakiness was abating. Closing my eyes, I thought of everything that had happened since I'd found my mother's dress destroyed.

Was it real?

Was any of this real?

After replaying everything in my head, I felt exhausted. Getting to my feet, I made my way back into the sitting room. Opening the cupboard Beau had gone into, I poured myself another port, a large one, and then sat on the sofa. Everything mellowed further until the thought of his kiss on my lips was but a distant memory as exhaustion overtook me. Finishing off the remainder of the port in my glass, I pulled the blanket back over me and let my body be pulled under in sleep.

My eyes fluttered open but this time I wasn't looking at the ceiling. I'd moved onto my side and was staring at the back of the sofa. I was still at the castle. Touching my lips, I recalled how I'd moved towards Beau and kissed him. Did he resent me for it? He'd kissed me back, but maybe now, given time to consider things, he'd reject me. He wouldn't be the first, would he? The only person who'd loved me was now dead.

If Beau loved you, he's dead too, my mind considered. I shook off my thoughts. They were a waste of time. I had things to do today.

Turning around, the large clock on the mantle showed me it was just after seven am. I had hours until Beau would appear again. Hours to deal with the fact that fantasy appeared to be reality. Before I decided what to do with myself, I needed to get a wash and something to wear. It was time to go find my mum's suite of rooms. I made my way out into the hall.

"Morning, sweetie." Iris appeared at the side of me.

"Jesus, Iris." I clutched my chest.

"Sorry," she said, but mischief danced in her eyes, leading me to think she was anything but.

"How do you know Beau?" I quizzed. Maybe my first question to her should have been asking why she was here, but I was full of queries I wanted answers to, and that was the first that came out of my mouth.

"I've bought furniture and paintings from him in the past. Your mum got him into selling some of the house's antiques to raise funds for the upkeep of the place, but of course she could only help him sell to the humans. He knew he'd make more money dealing with the fae. I became fond of your mother, even though I did not know her for long, so when Beau asked me if I could help with the ball, I agreed."

"If it hadn't been so sudden, do you think he would have turned her?" I asked.

"Hmm," she pondered. "I think that's a question you need to ask Beau directly, but personally, I don't think he would have. Because if your mum wanted to be a vampire, she could have asked him to sire her while she was alive."

"I will ask him."

"I'm sure you will, along with another million questions while your mind assimilates with the fact all you're experiencing is real. Now," she said. "Let me take you to your mother's rooms. I'm guessing you were headed there anyway?"

"Yes. I need something to wear so that I can go out to buy food, and no, I don't want any of *your* food."

She smirked. "I didn't bring you any."

I paused to examine Iris. "Why are you helping me?"

"Because I liked your mum. Think of me as your faerie godmother. I'll be around today to show you what your mum left you, and tell you what she did around the place, how it all worked. Then I'll leave you in peace." She reached into her pocket and took out a black velvet pouch. "Inside here is a small sphere of Tiger's Eye on a pendant. Hold the sphere within your palm and say 'Iris help' three times and I will come to you when I can."

She took the pendant from the pouch and helped fasten it around my neck.

"It will not break," she said, answering a question I'd thought of but had yet to ask.

"Can you read my mind too?" I queried.

"No, it's just a natural question that comes up. Not my first rodeo at being a faerie godmother." She headed towards the bottom of the large staircase. "Right, come on. Let's show you what you've got."

The house was full of dark cherry wood doors, coving and dado rails, balustrades, and doorframes. There was black painted furniture and orangey-red carpets. Simple ironwork adorned the lighting. There was one chandelier that hung in the hallway. That was all. We passed underneath it as we took the staircase. I followed Iris as she turned left and walked down a corridor for a minute until we reached a door. It was strange to think my mum had trod this same path many times.

"Ready?" she asked.

I nodded.

Pushing open the door, I found the room in darkness. Iris moved over to the windows and opened the curtains. Thick black velvet had covered them. No wonder it had been so dark.

"Beau insisted the curtains remain closed until you entered the room. Now these rooms are yours to do with as you please. But these aren't your rooms to stay in. Those are further down. He didn't feel you'd want to sleep where your mother did, so you have other rooms here, although it's your choice."

I took in a large inhale. He had been very considerate of my needs, of my emotions. Once more I recollected his lips on mine. *Keep mindful of where you are now*, I chastised myself.

The first room we had entered was a sitting room. There was a threadbare grey sofa and a scuffed black coffee table. The carpet was also grey and clearly worn in places. But everywhere I looked there was fabric and lengths of ribbon. The coffee table housed a sewing machine, and a half-finished dress was draped across the back of the sofa.

At the rear of the room was another door. Opening that revealed my mum's bedroom. An ornate four-poster was covered in a beautiful blanket that my mum had clearly fashioned from spare pieces of fabric. She'd made sheets and matching pillowcases in a cream cotton. At this point I wished Iris wasn't here, because I wanted to lie on the bed and see if I could breathe in my mother's scent. But there would be time for that later. Right now, I should be grateful I had a guide for this huge castle.

Opening her wardrobe, I found a few simple dresses hung there and one more elaborate one.

"The dresses she made for you are elsewhere. I will take you shortly," Iris said.

Other than these two rooms there was just a small bathroom.

"Okay, I've seen enough. I'll come back later. Could you show me my rooms now please?" I asked.

We re-traced our steps and then walked further down the hall until we came to the very last door. Pushing open the door of that room, I gasped.

It had been painted. The walls were cream, the woodwork bright white. Though the furniture was still old it had clearly been stripped, sanded, and varnished. A cover had been made for the sofa in a beige damask fabric. But what had made me gasp was the light that came into the room from the huge windows. As an end room, it looked out over the castle grounds, over the mass of trees that seemed to go on endlessly. Neat curtains were hung at the windows.

"My mother did all this for me coming here, didn't she?"

"Yes. She used her evenings to focus on what you'd need when you got here. Used her small amount of wages to buy surplus materials for a good price."

Repeating what I'd done in my mum's rooms, I walked over and pushed open the bedroom door. Again, there was a four-poster bed, but this one was draped with a canopy. She'd made the bedding for this one too. And on this occasion when I pulled open the wardrobe door, dress after dress hung there. Some plain, some more sophisticated.

I dropped to my knees, fondling the fabric of one of the dresses. Apart from her chores she must have never stopped making things, mainly for me.

"Was she happy here?" I'd asked Beau this, but I wanted a second opinion. Reassurance.

"She was, Ella. Very much so. She had shadows under her eyes from being apart from you, but otherwise she was quite content. She lived for the day she got you back and prepared accordingly."

"But then she never got me back. Not in life," I noted, my posture slumping.

Iris came and sat next to me and took hold of my hand.

"You got to say goodbye. Not everyone gets that."

We were silent for a moment while I composed my fraught emotions.

"Did she say what she thought might happen when we reunited? Did she have any plans?"

"Only for you to stay here until you'd decided what you wished to do."

Her responses were basically the same as Beau's. Either they were both hoodwinking me, or it was the truth, and it did feel genuine in my gut.

Getting back to my feet, I selected one of the dresses and pushed open the bathroom door. It was clean and tidy in there and I washed my face, finding some products in the mirrored cupboard above the sink. I removed my sheet dress, exchanging it for the dress mum had made me. It wasn't an exact fit, but it was near enough. A little roomy on the bust, a little tight on the butt. Later I could try them all and see which fit best, but for now this beige cotton dress with a white lace collar would do.

"I will leave my mum's rooms as a place to visit to feel close to her for now," I stated. "I will stay here in these rooms."

"As you wish. Okay, let me show you the main rooms of the castle and then I'll leave you to do whatever it is you feel like doing."

And that's what she did. She showed me where Beau's rooms were on the other side of the main staircase, showed me the kitchen and pantries again. The dining room. A garden room at the back where plants had gone rogue inside and outside of it. The door through the garden room led out onto a patio where weeds grew through cracks in the concrete and slabs. Beyond was a garden that in the past would have been stunning, but now the grass was apparently mowed fortnightly and that was it. The shrubs were overgrown and straggly, the odd flower appearing on a wilting stem. Beyond that was the woodland. A dense canopy of trees causing shade.

Back inside, there was a library, a study, another sitting room covered in cloths and unused. We walked past many rooms Iris said were unused. She concentrated on the ones I needed to know. A guest bathroom. A small cloakroom.

"Is there any money for shopping in the house do you know?" I knew I needed more than pasta and sauce. There was no milk for potential visitors either, though did Beau actually receive any?

"It would be in that butter dish there on the side if there is any."

I lifted it up and sure enough there was about thirty pounds there in notes and change.

"I think that's everything, but you have your pendant if you need me for anything else." Iris squeezed my arm.

"It's so very hard not to say thank you for everything you've done. So would you like anything my mum left behind, other than her clothes? It would be a gift from my mum, not me."

"Would I be able to have her bedspread?" Her eyes lit up. "Only we chatted often while she made them. It would remind me of her dearly."

"You can have the one from my bed, as I should like the one from my mother's. Take it with you."

"Are you sure?"

"I am. It says everything I'm unable to say. Mum would want you to have a reminder of your friendship."

I gave the small woman a hug and then she scurried out of the room, wiping her eyes, and I heard her light footfall climbing the stairs.

Taking the money from the dish, I realised I had no shoes or a coat.

"Goddamn it," I shouted.

"You okay?" Iris' voice came from the hall.

"Oh sorry, I thought you'd gone?"

"Just on my way when I heard your voice. Problem?"

"Only that I have no footwear or a coat, and I want to get out of this bloody house."

She laughed. "I can help you but it's only temporary. I can glamour, remember?"

She picked up a pair of salt and pepper shakers and shook them. The next thing, she had two trainers in her hands. "Not a great look with the dress, but better for the walk."

I took them from her and put them on. They fit perfectly.

She then swept the tablecloth off the table and shook that. A moment later I had a coat and a matching tote for carrying some shopping in. A gravy boat became a handbag and the butter dish a purse for the money.

"Remember, at midnight, these return to what they were. Oh, and if you happen to return to your house, all the doors inside were unlocked by Beau before he left. And just so no one sees you there, the coat will cloak you, so keep it on if you go back to Poplar."

"I'm invisible?"

Iris giggled.

"No, but anyone who sees you will see a woman but not identify who it is."

"Phew. Didn't want to have my shopping looking like it was getting to the counter on its own."

We both chuckled and Iris left properly this time. I went out of the garden room door, locking it and taking the key with me, and then I walked around the front of the house and started the long journey back to the village.

It would give me time to think some more, now I was alone with my thoughts.

CHAPTER 10

ELLA

I actually enjoyed the walk to the village. Seeing the scenery in the daylight. There was something about the long driveway and its surrounding greenery I found comforting, and I pictured my mum doing the same walk.

And I was free. No more father, or stepfamily.

I should have felt guilty about his death, about their punishments, but I didn't. My father had broken my heart and my will and there was nothing left to mourn him with. Instead, I was relieved, almost... happy, that he wasn't around anymore.

There was clearly something wrong with me in the head. Maybe I had indeed developed a familial madness. If so, I was embracing it, because this Ella was able to swing her handbag and sing as she walked to the shops.

I began singing *Hickory Dickory Dock*, my favourite nursery rhyme taught to me by my mother, but I changed the words to suit myself.

Hickory Dickory Dock
My family liked to mock
The clock struck twelve
On the mantle shelf
And Ella took revenge on the lot.

I hummed and sang until I eventually reached the shops. I pushed open the door, hearing the bell ring, and a shopkeeper looked over and smiled. "Good morning. Or is it afternoon? Oh it is, just."

"Good afternoon," I said, picking up a basket and striding with purpose to the first aisle. No more leftovers. I chose the food I wanted to eat. If it wasn't for a lack of money and having to carry it, I would have filled twenty baskets. Soup, fruit, chocolate, slices of beef, potatoes, peas, and carrots, and a few more essentials. I counted up as I went along and had spent all but a few pence of what I'd brought.

But it felt good. I'd been seen and acknowledged and passed a few polite sentences in chit chat with the shopkeeper. There was some irony in the fact my parents' deaths meant I was coming to life.

From there, I went back to the place that had once been my home. I opened the back door and went inside. I'd expected to see evidence of police inspection, but of course Beau had taken care of that. It meant I could walk around the house at my leisure, seeing what I could take with me.

The first thing I did was get a large suitcase out of the cloakroom. I carried it upstairs where I unzipped it on the landing and left it open wide. Going into my father's room, I stood for a moment taking in the sheer luxury he and Glennis had enjoyed while I'd laid on a thin mattress in the cellar.

I imagined it was me at his jugular, ripping into his flesh instead of Beau. Right now, I wouldn't be surprised if my muscles and veins strained against my skin like the Hulk. Taking a deep breath, I reminded myself that I wasn't here for this. To punish myself for what I'd not been given. I was here to take what I needed and then to turn my back on this place forevermore.

Opening my stepmother's wardrobe door, I knew I wanted none of her clothes, but her jewellery was in here. I picked out every piece, putting it inside some of her more expensive designer handbags and walked out of the room placing them in the case. Maybe I would need to return until I'd taken all the valuables I could sell out of the house? I'd ask Beau to help. His being able to travel quickly would move things in half the time and we could split the profits so he and the castle could benefit.

Having decided that, I didn't worry about packing any further handbags and chose a couple of pairs of Glennis' shoes that would do until I had money of my own to spend. Then I moved to my father's side of the wardrobes. Moving the suits to one side, I stared at the safe. I only knew it was here because I'd heard Glennis moaning about my dad not trusting her with the passcode when I'd been cleaning upstairs once. I'd smiled smugly when he'd told her she could ask for anything she wanted and so didn't need to know what was inside.

I tried all their dates of birth, my date of birth, my mother's date of birth even, but nothing worked. Then I randomly placed numbers before banging my fist on it in frustration because it still didn't open. Leaving the room, I went around the rest of the house taking inventory of everything that could be easily removed.

Ready to leave, with not that much in the case given I planned to return with Beau, I walked back into the bedroom and faced the safe. *Come on, Ella, was there a number or date important to him?*

My mind wandered back to my childhood.

"Hi, Daddy. Did you have a good day at work?"

"Yes, Ella, I did. And do you know why?"

I did because he said it every time I asked.

"Because I'm number one, and so everyone wants to make me happy. Remember that in life, Ella. Remember number one."

It couldn't be that simple, could it? No one was that stupid, surely. The code was six digits. I pressed 1-1-1-1-1-1. Beep. It opened. Dad had clearly banked on Glennis not thinking it would be anything that easy.

Grabbing the edge of the door to pull it open, I stared at the contents. Money. Lots and lots of bundles of money. I took them out and stuffed them in the case. Then putting a couple of the notes in my purse and hoping it wasn't counterfeit or similar, I carried my bags, left the house, and pulled my case further down the street where I waved down a cab.

I refused the taxi drivers help and pulled the case alongside me in the back of the car. "Moonstone Castle, please," I directed.

"Moonstone Castle? Gosh, I've never been there before. You staying there?" the driver asked, a middle-aged man with sandy-coloured hair and glasses. His voice held genuine interest rather than the polite chatter I expected he rolled out to passengers as a rule.

"Yes, I'm a guest of Mr Salinger," I replied, because saying I was the new help didn't really add up to the fact I had a Louis Vuitton suitcase beside me in the back of the taxi.

"What's he like? Rumours always say he's dour and unfriendly."

I met the driver's gaze through his rear-view mirror. "That's just jealousy. He's a dear. Very reclusive though. I'm lucky to have received an invitation. It's only because I've offered to oversee some renovations."

"God, bet it takes some upkeep, a castle."

"Indeed."

He twittered on about some programme he'd seen on the television about renovating a French chateau until we pulled up outside of the castle. As he remarked about its imposing façade, it was like I was looking at it for the first time, which in some ways I guess I was, given I'd only seen it in the dark.

I paid the taxi driver and watched him disappear out of view, then carrying my goods, I went around the back once more and entered through the garden room. I unpacked the food in the kitchen and put it away, and then finally, I reached my bedroom, where I cast my belongings on the floor, and threw myself onto the sofa.

Looking at the clock, I sighed. There was still a number of hours yet until Beau might surface. I'd get something to eat, having missed lunch, and then I'd go wandering in the garden and go look at the woods, reminding myself my trainers were still good until midnight.

Once more I left through the garden room and this time I walked the length of the garden until the woods appeared. There was a wider path, just hard earth, with little offshoots in different directions. Sticking to the main path, I ambled along, knowing there was no rush whatsoever. Plus, I needed to ensure I didn't trip on any tree roots which had spread through the path in places. While a lot of the woodland had been left to grow wild, this main path had been kept tidy. Had my mother walked this same terrain? Had she ventured into the woods like I was doing now or had she preferred to feel safe within the castle itself? I'd ask Beau sometime. Personally, I loved the solidity of the earth under my feet, and the feel of bark under my hands when I felt drawn to touch an old, established tree.

As I continued my adventure, insects dotted around, and spiders darted away as I damaged their webs with my hands if it brushed my face. I'd been walking for what felt like twenty minutes when a stream appeared, the sound of the water soothing to my ears. It ran not too far from the path, so I continued the same way. Eventually, the stream grew wider until it became a small river. And at one part of it there was a small wooden bench, but that wasn't the thing that caught my eye the most. No, the thing that caught my eye was a large, rusted birdcage. Whether it had genuinely been an aviary or whether it was just a garden ornament or antique, I couldn't be sure, but it was huge. I could easily fit inside it myself. Vines and brambles twisted within it. The whole thing needed a clean-up and to be repainted, and I decided to ask Beau if I could do it. I knew there were many more things I needed to get done as part of my work, but I would do this in my spare time. Walking around it, picking off bits of vine and bramble, some that were sharp and bit into my hands making them sore, I wondered just what it was about the cage that I liked. I'd never been into birds, or antiques, but there was just *something* about it.

When I finally determined what it was, it shocked me slightly. It reminded me of my room in the cellar. Of safety. Though it had been my prison, it had also been my place of respite, my escape.

I laughed to myself. Finally free and admiring a cage! Moving away from it, I sat on the bench and watched the water run down the river, and I thought about anything and everything as I sat there, including the fact this wasn't dissimilar to my fantasy of a picnic by a lake with a lover. Alas, the man I'd recently kissed could not sit with me under the glare of the sun.

"If I didn't have my scenting abilities, I would have wondered where you'd got to," a familiar voice said once dusk had fallen. I turned my head slightly and smiled at him. I'd been wondering if he'd come here since the light had begun to dim, but I'd been enjoying the fresh air and views too much to make my way back inside.

"Good evening, Beau. Sleep well?" I asked him, watching as he came to sit beside me.

"Not as well as usual, no. I found myself dreaming of a beautiful blonde woman. She became an angel who wanted to embrace her inner hidden demons."

"I might just be the woman who saves you, Beau," I remarked, and he startled slightly.

"Saves me? I wasn't aware I needed saving."

"Correction. Not you per se, but I appear to have come into a small fortune," I said, and I brought him up to speed with what was at the house.

"Do you have plans this evening, or would you like to collect the rest of your belongings?" he asked, winking.

I thought he may spirit me to the house and back in the vampire way, but instead he went into a garage and brought out a small van. The white of it was filthy, but I smirked and said, "Who'd have thought, Beau, the dark prince, also masqueraded as a 'white van man'."

"You really need to leave your fictional assumptions about vampires behind," he said, shaking his head. "We have to reside among the living, to blend in. It is in private that our true selves show."

His words made a shiver run down my spine and then he smirked.

I rolled my eyes at him.

"Are you going to get in then or are you walking there?" he teased playfully.

Eye-rolling a second time, I opened the passenger door and climbed inside.

"How did you spend your day? Any questions come to light?" Beau asked as we travelled down the lane towards the main village.

"Iris arrived and showed me around the castle. Then I went food shopping and to the house. Finally, I explored the woodland. And yes, I have two questions. Firstly, may I restore the birdcage?"

"If you're staying, then be my guest. And your second question?"

"Do you regret kissing me back?"

He stopped the van. It wasn't an immediate braking, but it was enough I shunted forwards against my seatbelt a little.

"Not in the slightest," he answered. "Since I saw you at the river all I've wanted to do is claim your mouth again and claim elsewhere. The second you give me permission, I'm going to take you to bed and your question of do I regret kissing you back will be answered beyond doubt."

My breath quickened and I became acutely aware of my breasts rising and falling.

"Right, let's get moving again," Beau said. "Before burglars beat us to it."

And acting like he hadn't just said he'd like to take my virginity and possess me, he continued driving to the house.

If anyone noticed us going in and out of the house, they didn't approach us. I was unaware if the news of the deaths would have reached the neighbourhood given the police had been enthralled. Even if it had, I was just a daughter collecting her possessions, and if anyone did come snooping about potential gossip, my vampire companion would have sent them on their way with lies in their mind.

"I will take your word for the value of the jewellery, shoes, and bags etc," Beau said. "But I shall presume the ornaments and paintings are all likely of extreme value."

"If I could, I'd sell everything in here," I stated. "However, I shall leave the furniture and furnishings behind to gather dust. We'll have more than enough money in everything we'll have collected to last for years, probably for my whole lifetime."

Beau stared at me for a moment too long and I wondered what he was thinking, but then he moved onto collecting more things.

Was he imagining me not being human, but a vampire like him?

I wasn't sure how I felt about that. All I knew was I was excited by the situation I found myself in: with rooms in a beautiful house, my mother's things close. Now with money. And in the company of a man I found intriguing and beguiling.

Maybe he's enthralling you? I thought. Then I decided if he was, I didn't care.

We made two trips in all, dropping everything off in the banqueting hall for the time being.

As I walked away from the family home for what could be the final time, I silently thanked it for the good times, and then turned my back on the place. Whatever happened in my future, I doubted I would ever come back here.

I was silent for much of the drive back, as the full realisation hit that I was no longer a captive in my old home. Once I had money, I could do anything I wanted. I was free.

So the irony that right now I wanted to do nothing but stay at Moonstone Castle made me chuckle.

Beau's eyes cast upon me for a moment before he looked back at the road again.

"Might I ask what is amusing you right now?" he enquired.

"That I can go wherever I want, and yet I want to stay at the castle... with you..." I replied, before adding, "...the creep from the park."

He laughed alongside me.

CHAPTER 11

BEAU

I f only Ella knew how hard it was for me to walk up to her softly by the side of the river. How the beast within me wished to grab her by the hair, bite her neck and suck her into submission, before roughly entering and claiming her.

Now her thoughts were blocked from me, I had no idea how she saw me, but if it were through rose-tinted spectacles, she needed to realise that the tint in reality was splattered blood.

She was speaking of staying in the castle. Wanted to spend time with the stranger she'd met in the park. And despite my knowing she should be making the most of her freedom, I wanted her to stay, if only for what was an eyeblink of time in my endless existence.

I had made sure to feed well before we journeyed to

her previous home, and yet her scent still pervaded every pore of my flesh. My eyes roamed over her body when she wasn't looking, taking in the swell of her breasts and the curve of her hips. I wanted to spill inside her, claim her, impregnate her. My wish for children was strong within me, a torturous cry for continuity, and my biology had found its perfect vessel —Ella.

How I didn't crash the van while all this whirled within me, I didn't know. But I eventually reached the castle, and we carried our treasure into the hall. I showed off, moving at lightning speed and depositing the items much faster than Ella could. It annoyed her immensely. I could see it in the slight jut of her jaw. She was competitive and hated feeling inferior. I understood. She'd been made to feel that way for the past six years.

"That's everything." I stood back from the piles of items and addressed Ella. "I will leave you to organise the sales of what you wish, and Iris will help you as she did your mother. Shall we retire to the sitting room for a while now?"

"Yes. If you'll excuse me, I'm going to fix myself a coffee and a slice of cake. I'll join you there."

I nodded and made my way to the sitting room

where a few minutes later the smell of coffee pervaded the room.

Ella devoured the slice of vanilla sponge as I'd envisaged snacking on her neck. It reminded me of what she'd been denied over the past years of her life. The little moans that escaped her mouth made my cock hard to the point I had to quickly leave the room, or the cup and plate were going to be knocked from her hands.

And that's where she found me. Outside of the room, leaning against the wall, battling with my desire to have her.

I shook my head. "Go back in the room, Ella."

"Why?" she challenged. Always so impudent.

"*Go back in the room!*" I ordered. "Or you'll be in my bed. Simple as that."

Instead of retreating, she walked towards me.

Permission granted.

She'd had her chance to deny. Now it was gone. Any protests would fall on deaf ears as my thirst took away my humanity.

I swept her up and flew straight to my rooms. The doors were rattled on their hinges as my impatience to bed her threatened my very sanity.

She bounced on my bed as I threw her down on it,

and if she didn't bounce herself upon it several times more, teasing me as her tits rose and fell.

"I forgot what a soft mattress was like," she commented. "I look forward to you deflowering me upon it."

God, this woman. She should be petrified, and yet her eyes shone with desire. I commented as much. "Why are you not afraid of me?"

"Maybe I am afraid. It's just I've discovered I seem to dance at the edge of darkness, and you've invited me to tango."

I tore the clothes from her body until she was completely bare to me, and then I shed my own. Her eyes gazed hungrily at my torso and my cock.

"I want to touch you." Her fingers reached out, but I kept my distance.

"Don't worry, you'll have your chance," I told her. "But first, I need to taste your skin."

I moved above her and stared deep into her eyes. Her own blinked rapidly, the only physical giveaway to any nervousness, because her heart beating wildly could be that or simple desire.

I swept my face closer and brushed my mouth against hers. Once, twice, and then possessively. She answered my kiss with her own hunger. I plunged my tongue inside her mouth, tangling it with her own. My hands fastened in her hair possessively, bringing her head up to mine. We kissed until my need for more made me break off. My mouth moved down her collarbone where I allowed myself to snuffle a little. That was for later though. For now, I kissed and trailed my tongue all over her body taking in the salty taste of her flesh. Her skin goose bumped as I worked my way around her, deliberately ignoring the most erogenous of zones until I'd tasted every other bit of her. Moving back up her body from her delicate ankles, I fastened my mouth over her right breast. She moaned wildly. "Oh my god."

I knew no one had been here before and if that didn't make me even harder. My burgeoning cock was purple and straining against her thigh. I lightly nipped at her hardened nipple before moving to the other. My fangs grazed but didn't puncture.

"Have you ever explored yourself with your own fingers?" I asked her.

"Yes," she said breathily.

That was all I needed to hear to decide to move on to the next level of exploration. I moved down, pushing her thighs apart and licking my lips at the sight of her wet folds. Then I licked up her seam.

She almost threw me off the bed as she bucked wildly. "What the—"

I gazed up at her from between her legs and laughed at her shocked face. "Oh, Ella, you have so much to enjoy."

I returned, being gentle with my tongue until she became used to the sensation. As she began to moan and writhe and beg for more, I entered her with my tongue and used my fingers against her clit until eventually she detonated against my mouth. There was no other word for it. Tremors shook her body from head to toe as she shuddered against me. I sucked on her essence greedily. Her wetness divine.

Then while she was so sated, I nudged against her entrance.

Her eyes widened. "What about birth control?"

"I will withdraw on this occasion," I informed her. "But this is the only time, Ella. I want my cum inside you. I want your tummy rounded with my child. The next time we fuck you'll be filled with it. Or it won't happen again."

Then I thrust inside her so that I didn't have to see the answer in her eyes, because I feared it wouldn't be the one I wanted.

"It hurts a little," she said.

"It won't in a moment," I told her and then I moved the hair away from her neck and nuzzled against her. She shivered against me and then I bit down. The sweet taste of her on my tongue was everything and more, like she was a wine whose grapes had been grown to my every specification and fermented to my exact recipe. I took just enough even though I wanted *more*. At the same time my cock rode her, while her hips raised and she greedily began pushing against me, riding me, chasing her climax.

"Beau. Oh fuck, oh fuck."

Breaking off the bite and licking it closed, I moved us so that one of her legs was positioned around my hip, and I knelt and thrust inside her until I could wait no longer, and neither could she. As I felt her ripple around my cock and gasp as if it were her last grip on the edge of a mountain before she fell, fell, fell, I withdrew and pumped my cock so I came all over her stomach.

Then I sat back and watched her come down from her climaxes and come back to the real world.

"Let me get a washcloth," I said, excusing myself from the bed. I quickly washed myself in my bathroom and then dampened a couple of washcloths, carrying those and a towel into the room.

She watched as I cleaned her up.

"So that's what is inside of a man's cock," she said.

"Yes."

"And that carries your seed? Same as a human man?"

"Yes, except a human man is fertile from puberty. I am fertile only at certain times in my undead life."

"And one of those times is now?" she asked.

"Yes."

"Did you mean what you said? That you won't use protection or come on my stomach again? I mean, wasn't it enjoyable?"

"It was immensely enjoyable, my dear Ella, and were I human I would take you over and over again, but I'm not, and you need to allow yourself to accept what I truly am. I have needs and desires that go beyond an enjoyable dalliance." I moved in closer to her, letting my true nature in a little more, knowing my eyes would be a deep ruby red. "My nature wishes to consume you body and soul, Ella. I want to turn you into my mate, fuck you and make love to you over and over again. Chain you to this castle so that you can't leave. Have you bear my children. Not one, Ella. I want my own brood, my own nest. The Salingers. So, from now on, I will make you come as much as you like, but I will not fuck you again. Not unless you're ready to accept my seed."

She opened her mouth to speak, but I leaned over her and kissed any words away. "There are no decisions to be made now, Ella. It is too soon. I wouldn't let you say yes right now anyway. Not until I knew beyond a doubt that you were sure. This is not blackmail, rather just simple biology. To waste my seed hurts me. Cleaning it off you cut me deep. My potential wasted."

I kissed her more.

"But I can't regret having possessed you, Ella. The trouble is, I feel you've possessed me too." I kissed her a final time, then I gathered her into my arms and carried her down to her own room.

"My apologies about your dress. I know your mother sewed it for you, but—"

"She made me plenty, and that one did not fit so well. But next time, I'll strip okay?"

"Next time?"

"If you think I'm satisfied with only one tryst with that talented tongue of yours, you are very much mistaken," she said.

"Hmm," I perused, before laying her gently upon her bedsheets. "I think I may do it again right now to help you settle off to sleep."

I took my sweet time, licking and teasing until I brought her off once more. This time her own fingers clutched my hair as her confidence grew and she pulled me nearer so she could ride my face. When she came, I kissed her goodnight, so she could taste herself on my tongue, and then I left her room and went back to my suite to work on my own chores of the day.

But I found it hard to concentrate because all I could think of was *Ella, Ella, Ella*. In my home, in my bed, carrying my baby.

Frustrated, because I knew what I had to do next and knowing I didn't want to, I picked up the empty bottle of blood I'd consumed and I hurled it at the wall, watching it shatter like my unbeating heart.

CHAPTER 12

ELLA

He left me, and at first, I felt sated, satisfied, and exhausted.

I was consumed by re-running everything he'd done in my head over and over, taking in the sensations of the slight chafing on my breasts, the soreness between my legs, the puffiness of my lips where they'd been kissed repeatedly. My fingers went to my neck but there wasn't even a tenderness there.

Climbing off my bed, wondering if the drowsiness was from Beau tasting my blood or from the sex, I walked into my bathroom and stared in the bathroom mirror. I looked no different. I'd expected a paler pallor but with rosy-red cheeks. My usual porcelain skin, blue eyes, and pink mouth faced me, though my lips were definitely a little swollen.

Turning on the shower, I washed myself thoroughly, dried my body and hair, and then dressed in some pyjamas made by my mum, before turning back the sheets. I climbed inside and pulled up the sheet and blanket, closed my eyes and waited for sleep to claim me.

I waited... and waited... but despite feeling shattered, sleep would not come. The mattress was too damn soft, and all the covers felt stifling.

Annoyed, I kicked off the covers and carrying my blanket I took myself downstairs to the sitting room where I'd fallen asleep the night before. I quickly drank down a port in case that might help and then laid on the sofa. I'd just drift off and then I'd get uncomfortable again. By this time, dawn was breaking, and I was so tired I could have cried. Leaving the room with my blanket around my shoulders, I went and got myself a glass of milk and then I walked to the garden room, pushed open the doors and went outside. I knew where I was headed and sure enough, I didn't stop until I came to the bench, the river, and the birdcage. Pushing open the door of the birdcage, I pushed away the bramble using the edge of the blanket until there was a space large enough for it. I placed it down, laid on half and pulled the other half over myself. It was hard and uncomfortable, but I was asleep before I could have counted to five.

It was Iris who found me there. I woke, rubbed my eyes and had no idea of where I was. Not the birdcage and not even the castle.

"What on earth are you doing out here? It isn't safe, child, to be out in the castle grounds in the open like this."

"I couldn't sleep. This was the only place. Everywhere was too comfortable."

She smiled. "Our very own princess and the pea, except you actually want the peas."

I stood up and exited the birdcage. "How ridiculous, that I couldn't sleep in a comfy bed."

"No, it's not. You've known a different reality for six years. It will take time to get used to new things. It's only your second full day here, Ella."

She took my hand. "Come on, let's get you a nice strong coffee, shall we? Then a good breakfast. After that, let's take a look at everything you brought from your old home."

I turned to her quickly. "Beau told you?"

"Yes. He wants you to open a bank account and have savings as soon as possible."

"I need my birth certificate to open a bank account. I've no idea where that is."

"It was in your mother's drawer in her bedside table. Now it's in your room. I left it there when I came to find you and you were gone."

"How did you know where I'd be?"

"Beau told me that you'd been here when he'd woken yesterday."

"Does he tell you everything?" I snapped before regretting my actions. "Sorry, that was uncalled for."

"No, he doesn't. But your current actions and body language are telling me a lot. Beau is a good man. But don't rush into anything, Ella. You only just got your freedom, don't immediately tie yourself down."

I nodded, but I knew I looked sullen, like my stepsisters denied what they wanted at that moment in time.

"You can have lots of fun without being tied down," Iris noted. "Actually, you can have lots of fun being tied down too." She winked and I laughed, the awkwardness gone.

"Come now, let's get that coffee, and the twigs out of your hair," she said, pulling one free and laughing at me.

Iris helped me to make an inventory of the things from my old home. She was extremely knowledgeable with antiques and designer goods and there were only a few things she needed to research more. She asked for the fae to have first refusal on the items which I agreed to. When she'd gone, I called the bank and asked about setting up a bank account. They'd had a cancellation and so early that afternoon I found myself in an appointment with a banking assistant explaining that until I'd reached eighteen my strict parents had not allowed me any financial freedom.

"I came into some money on my eighteenth birthday that I would like to deposit," I told the assistant.

He went through what the checks would be and with that I returned to the castle. On my way back I popped into a shop that sold gardening and other household items and purchased the things I needed to start on the birdcage.

I'd totalled the money up I'd brought from the safe and there was over a hundred thousand pounds. I needed to ask Beau if there was somewhere I could keep it safe, but be able to access it, until such time as all the checks on my account were completed and I could deposit it.

Remembering that of course my residence here was subject to me keeping the house in order, I next cleaned the sitting room and then the kitchen. When Beau was up, I would go clean his own rooms.

Finally, with all my tasks done, I made my way back to the birdcage armed with long gardening gloves, dressed in some overalls I'd purchased, and with thick black sacks, secateurs, and a small saw. I cleared the cage of bramble and weeds as far as I could reach. Even the thick bags tore in places due to the thorns and I still managed to get a few scratches, but on the whole, the gloves and overalls did their job and I freed up the bottom two-thirds of the cage. As the dusk descended, I made my way back to the house, grabbed a shower, and then waited for Beau in the sitting room.

"Good evening, Ella. How has your day been?" he asked as he walked into the room. Desire swam through my veins. I wanted more of what he'd given me yesterday.

"I'm well. Thank you."

He sniffed at the air and then dove towards me,

lifting up my ankle and seeing the spots of dried blood there. He licked across the wound, finding any others and doing the same. They healed over following his touch.

"God, how I wish to taste you again, but you humans are so frail. It would weaken you too much. In a few days maybe, if you'd like."

I lifted the skirt of my dress up further revealing the top of my thighs and the fact I was wearing no panties. "You can taste something else; it doesn't have to be my blood this evening."

He made me come right there on the sofa in the sitting room. I wanted to repay the favour, wanted to touch him and learn how to work him with my hands, my mouth. Let him sink deep within me, but I knew the answer would be no.

Languishing on the sofa together afterwards, I told him how I'd been unable to sleep.

"You slept in the birdcage?"

"I did, and I know it was foolish, that I could have been attacked, but it was the only place I managed to fall asleep."

"You'll get used to your bed eventually."

"Yes, Iris said the same thing. But for now, looks like I might have to sleep on the floor!"

"You said you cleared most of the bramble off it?"

"Yes."

"Follow me, Miss Story," he said, and he set me to my feet. I followed him outside where he picked me up and took me to the river. There I watched as he quickly stripped the rest of the birdcage of its overgrowth.

"The cage is in four parts. If it's not too delicate or rusted, I have an idea," he told me. He rose off his feet to the top of it and eventually he managed to take it apart.

"I'm going to get you back to the manor, and we'll make some space in your room," he said. I just nodded and let him take the lead.

When he dropped me back at the door, Beau advised me to get some cleaning products together and then said he'd be back.

He eventually returned. "Bring the cleaning stuff to your rooms," he advised.

I carried my bucket and cloths up the stairs to my suite of rooms. Pushing open the door, I saw that Beau had re-arranged the room so that the bed was up against the wall in the corner and next to it was the enormous birdcage.

"Now you have a choice of where to sleep, but I know you'll be safe," he told me. "Pass me the bucket and I'll clean where you can't reach. Then you're on your own with it."

"Thank you, Beau."

He did as he said and then he went to leave.

"Beau?"

"Yes?"

"I want us to talk about the castle and what needs fixing. I have money now."

"Indeed. *You* have money."

"I live here, do I not?"

"You have rooms here because you work for me," he said delicately.

I huffed, annoyed.

"The garden room is overgrown and yet I think it could be my favourite room in the entire house. Can I have permission to refurbish it?"

"If you sell something from the house to pay for it."

I scowled at him. "That's ridiculous. I have enough money to do it. Why do I have to wait?"

"If I've learned anything in my years as a vampire it's that humans rush through life. Impulsively making decisions they regret not a moment later, and then of course it's too late. You have these rooms for you to do with as you wish, you have the birdcage to do with as you wish, you have more than enough household tasks to keep you occupied otherwise. But as for other things, you have to wait. Money doesn't afford you everything in life. Not when other people are involved, and I want to pay for my house myself. It's my home."

It's my home.

Not yours, was the intonation.

I was being ridiculous. I hardly knew him, hardly knew myself, and here I was demanding to redo rooms in his house like it was a large dolls house I'd been given.

But how did I explain that this felt like home already?

I didn't was the simple answer.

"You're right. I think my freedom is making me get ahead of myself and carried away. I will concentrate on the beautiful birdcage. I'm going to re-paint it as it was, cream. Where did it come from originally by the way?"

He shrugged his shoulders. "I don't know. It was here when I arrived. It's just a garden ornament, albeit on a large scale."

It wasn't an ornament to me. It represented a cage I was willing to put myself in. My choice.

"Right, I have some other matters to attend to. I shall bid you a good night," he said, and he left the room.

Over the next couple of weeks, I settled into a routine. I'd do housework or anything else Beau requested I do, such as go into town to pay some bills. I had coffee with Iris a couple of times a week. I still slept in the birdcage every night.

Beau had taken to bringing me up to my bedroom each evening and using his fingers and his mouth he would kiss me, tease me, please me, and leave me in my bed, thinking I'd be so relaxed I would finally sleep there. But every night I crawled out and back into the birdcage.

On this particular night, I was woken when my door creaked open.

"So here you are again, Ella. In the cage. Shall we get rid of the bed?"

I shuffled up as Beau entered the cage and laid beside me.

"No, because I have fun in the bed."

"You can have fun here."

His hands reached for the waistband of my pyjamas and pulled them lower so that his fingers could dip inside my wetness. He'd already brought me off twice earlier this evening, and now I was gasping again while his fingers dipped and darted.

"Beau, God, please."

"You're driving me to distraction," he whispered in

my ear. "Do you know how much I replay being inside you in my head? How I imagine you coming apart. You are killing me all over again."

"Then take me. You did it once," I pleaded. "I need you inside me."

"Will you bear my children?" he asked.

I paused.

"There will be no intercourse."

"I hadn't answered yet. I was thinking."

"That pause was your answer."

I pushed away from him. "I will make my own decisions, and if I say I've paused to think, then that's exactly what I've done," I snapped.

"I'm not going to fuck you tonight, Ella."

"I'd like you to leave now," I said, because I felt like I wanted to claw his eyes out. He got to taste me over and over. Three times now he'd enjoyed a few drops of my blood and he was forever satisfying my sexual desires. But I couldn't even touch him in return. It was pure torture.

Beau left the room once more and even though the cage usually brought a swift sleep, on this occasion it was a long while before I dropped off.

CHAPTER 13

BEAU

S he came apart in my arms, but she became alive day by day. She didn't see it. Didn't see the changes within her. Her sassy spirit had attracted me from the off, but that assertiveness and confidence had just grown and grown. She wanted to renovate my home, but it wasn't hers.

What I had to do next would cause her more hurt. I knew it. But sometimes you had to be cruel to be kind, and I didn't want a yes from someone who felt they didn't really have a choice.

I called her to my office the following day.

"I've come to a decision, Ella," I said. "I've decided

to sell Moonstone Castle and to move on. The repairs are never ending, and I don't use half of the place."

She stood like a statue for a moment. "W-what? You can't mean that."

My forehead wrinkled. "Why not? Vampires do move on. We live for many years and get bored. It's time for a change."

Those soft lips of hers pouted. "B-but I like it here. My mother lived here, and the river... my birdcage. I just got settled."

"You'll soon settle somewhere else," I replied indifferently.

Her lips were now pressed into a white slash. "Why are you really doing this? Is it because you're scared of what you feel for me?" she challenged.

She was so close to the truth, but I couldn't let her know that.

"What I feel for you? Ella, I've known you for three weeks."

Her hands came to her hips. "That's not true. You watched me for years."

I swept my hand dismissively. "Which as I've said to you before is a blink of the eye for a vampire. You're stuck here, Ella. You need to move on."

Drawing up to her full height, and lifting her chin,

she declared, "I've decided to be yours. I will bear your children."

"No."

"*What do you mean no*? That's what you said you wanted. We can be together. What the hell is wrong with you?" Spittle left her mouth as she raged at me. "You're being ridiculous. Why, Beau? Where has this come from? Talk to me. We can work it out."

"There's nothing left to say. I'm moving on. The end."

She argued until her frustration led to her storming out and slamming the door. In her fury, her heel got trapped in the doorway, and she left her shoe behind. I knew she'd be back later pleading with me again. But I wouldn't be here when she did. It was time to let my Ella out of the new cage we'd both put her in. And her shoe wouldn't be here either, because I would keep it as a reminder of her when she was gone.

CHAPTER 14

ELLA

Beau couldn't be serious. He was just panicking. And yes, I'd not expected my outburst about having his children, but I didn't want to lose him.

I ran out of the house and headed to the river where I sat on the bench and wept.

Finally, when I'd calmed down and worked out how I might negotiate with him to stay, I made my way back to the house. But a note pinned to his door said *Ella* simply on the front. I tore it down and opened it.

> My dearest Ella
> I do this not to be unkind. But because you mean so much. I did not get to live my whole human life. You have not got to live the last six years of it. You've never

*been able to be independent. You're hiding
here. So I've gone and it's time for you
to leave too. You have a bank account
filled with money and the whole world
available.*

*Your cage is no more so that you can
now fly.*
Beau

I dashed to my room for solace, storming through my living room and through to my bedroom. But when I opened the door, instead I shrieked. My birdcage was smashed to pieces. Completely destroyed. I'd thought he'd meant the 'cage' of Moonstone Castle, but no, he'd decimated my precious cage. My belongings were packed in my Louis Vuitton case, placed at the foot of the bed.

Sobbing, I clutched my Tiger's Eye pendant and shouted, "Iris help. Iris help. Iris help."

"I'm already here," she said, walking through from the living room. "I was in your sitting room but was my true fae size so you didn't see me."

"D-did *he* ask you to b-be here?"

"Yes." She drew in a breath. "He asked me to make sure you left."

As I noted her expression, I knew she was here to carry out his wishes. She'd known Beau far longer than my mother and me.

"I thought you were my faerie godmother. Shouldn't you make my wishes come true?"

"We all have your best interests at heart, Ella, and you need to leave." Though her tone was kindly, it still hurt like hell.

Anger pounded through my body, like my heart was a ticking bomb. I didn't say much more, I made sure my case held everything I required, and then I called for a taxi. I now had a mobile phone and though I didn't yet have a passport, I'd seen little of the U.K. I would get the taxi to the train station and get on the first train that arrived.

Finally, I stood in the doorway, the taxi idling at the kerb. "I wish you well, Iris."

She pulled me into her arms. "I'm sorry it had to be this way. But make the most of every minute, Ella, now you are truly free."

We broke apart and I got in the taxi. I didn't look back. My gaze stayed fixed ahead.

ANDIE M. LONG

Everything was strange. I felt so small in this large world of hustle and bustle. The taxi dropped me off at the train station and I stared at the departures list wondering where to go. Other travellers rushed around me, some running to make a train. I saw a mum berating her children to quit messing around. Saw the responsibility in her gaze to keep her kids safe. For a moment I wanted to run to her, to ask if she'd tell me what to do too.

I chose London first. Thought if nothing else, I could sightsee. Didn't envision the anxiety attack that would befall me the moment I stepped off the train.

As everyone piled off as the train terminated, a huge crowd formed at the ticket turnstiles. Shards of icy fear prickled at my back as I watched tickets be shown and the red cross or green tick appear. What if I fucked up and got the red cross and these passengers, all of whom seemed to be in a rush, tutted and complained about me?

My heart thudded in my chest, and I would have given anything to be able to run to the cellar for my safety, or to my birdcage, or the river. I still had the Tiger's Eye pendant around my neck, but there was no assistance from Iris to be found from it. However, the feel of it in my fingers was reassuring and I toyed with it while the queues went down, and with them, my heartbeat also lessened back to a steady rhythm.

By the time I booked myself into a hotel and reached my room I was mentally exhausted. Removing my coat, I threw myself down on the bed and I cried.

It hit me all at once: the loss of my mother, my freedom from my father and stepfamily, the weirdness of the time spent at Moonstone Castle when looked at objectively. It was like a rebirth as my tears washed away the grief, leaving me feeling like a brand-new version of myself. I guessed that's exactly what I was, an Ella free to do as she pleased.

For the next week, I stayed at the hotel and went from ordering room service, to taking tentative steps outside. I bought a travel guide and saw the sights like any other tourist in London, taking a tour bus that let you get on and off at various places. Getting braver, I ate alone in restaurants, and finally, I immersed myself in the crowds going shopping where I bought myself a silver chain that held a key. That day I took off the Tiger's Eye pendant and I threw it in a bin. Then I wrapped the key around my neck, the one that declared me free of all that other people had imposed on me.

I took myself to the Lake District next. It was so very different to where I'd just been. In Windermere, I got tickets for a boat trip where I sat and took in the scenery. I stayed in a hotel with amazing views. It was so quiet, but restful.

I stayed in the Lake District for a long time. There was something about the water that drew me to it like a moth to a flame. After taking a rental property, I applied for a passport, ordered travel guides, and began taking trips to other places in England and some small trips to Europe.

The first time I flew, I went to Paris. As the plane climbed high, I felt exhilarated, like I was flying at last, free as a bird. My mind would think of Beau, but I would quickly shut that down. He was in the past, and my feet were now planted firmly in the future.

And Paris was where I met my first lover.

"The view from up here is quite something," a man said. It took a moment before I realised he was talking to me.

I smiled at him in what I hoped was a polite manner. "Yes, I agree. Paris is such a pretty place."

"Oh I wasn't talking about Paris. I meant you."

I felt my cheeks heat.

He groaned. "Sorry, that was such a line. I wish I could take it back, but it's out there now. Too late. I'll leave you to get back to the view."

"No, that's okay." My words dashed out, scared otherwise he'd be gone. I was craving human company now, finally ready to do more than walk everywhere alone.

"Are you sure?" he double checked. "I'm not going to have an angry boyfriend come threaten to throw me off the tower?"

I laughed. "No boyfriend. You're quite safe." I quickly dismissed the vision of Beau that appeared in my mind. Of him dragging this man over the edge of the Tower, draining him as they plummeted, blood spilling like rubies falling from a shattered necklace.

The man came to stand beside me. His hair was blonde and his eyes grey. "I'm Leon," he said.

"Ella," I held out my hand for him to shake, but instead he brought it to his lips and kissed the back of it. His lips were cold from being outside and it reminded me once more of Beau. I swallowed. Was this how it always would be every time I met a man? It was time for me to wipe off all traces of the vampire and replace those memories with others.

Leon invited me for lunch, which continued on to

a visit to the Louvre, which led to dinner, and ended in Leon's hotel room. I did not want him in my room. That was still my sanctuary, my escape if needed. I'd slept with only one man, one time, and I didn't know if I would want to stay wrapped in Leon's arms afterwards or run like hell.

But Beau had started a thirst within me. Not for blood, but for the feeling of sated satisfaction that came after an orgasm. No matter what new experiences presented themselves, I relaxed at the touch of my fingers at my clit, and now I'd see what another man was like.

Leon stripped off his own clothes and gestured me for me to do the same. We climbed inside the covers and his hands roamed my body. As they did his breathing quickened. "Fuck, you're beautiful," he said, before enquiring about birth control.

"I'm on the pill but you need to wear a condom too," I told him. "I want no disease and certainly no children."

If he thought me cold, he said nothing, too overcome by lust to notice. There was little foreplay, but then that would have made me think of Beau, at the many times I'd come apart at the touch of his fingers and his tongue. As Leon penetrated me, and that was the word that sprang to mind because I was barely wet and the skin dragged, I was brought back to the current situation, and it was exactly what I needed. It was rough, animalistic almost, and I scratched at Leon's back as he ground himself against my pelvis. His fingers came to my clit as his pace built and I came almost as he did.

He turned onto his back, breathing heavily, and I looked at the sweat beaded across his brow. "I'm just going to clean up," he said, sitting up and moving to the bathroom.

I don't know what his thoughts would have been when he returned from the bathroom to find I'd left.

A taxi took me straight from his hotel to mine. I showered, put on my pyjamas, and watched a movie. Tomorrow I'd go back to my place in the Lakes.

CHAPTER 15

BEAU

I watched my beautiful captive fly free at last. Her confidence grew day by day, and I knew it was only a matter of time until she met a lover.

What I didn't know was that as I watched her from a distance follow the man into his hotel, it would hurt me more than my siring. But this was how it had to be, and so I continued to follow her and watch her live.

Over the next twelve years she explored the world. She studied interior design, and the international travel became for both business and pleasure as she flew to different clients and countries. Financially, she didn't need to work, but I saw the enjoyment she got from taking over a client's space and making it extra-ordinary. Ella got a reputation for her theatrical designs and in every one, somewhere, there featured a birdcage.

It was her signature move, whether a bird feeder hung from a tree or an elaborate candleholder. She also learned about antiques which married with her design business.

I was so very genuinely happy for her success, and yet I'd go home and scream where no one could hear me.

Every lover she took felt like a splash of holy water upon my skin.

But still, I couldn't regret what I'd done.

All I could do was wait and see if she ever came home to roost.

CHAPTER 16

ELLA

On my thirtieth birthday, I found myself back at a restaurant in Paris, the Eiffel Tower behind us through the window. I'd not been back since I'd met Leon, but my current boyfriend Patrick had whisked me away here for a romantic getaway.

We'd met at work as he'd employed me to do the interior design on his hotel based in Norfolk. It was near to the Broads, and I'd liked it there. A date had led to another and another, and before long I realised I had my first proper boyfriend. A committed relationship. Patrick was also an accomplished lover. Life was good and I had no complaints.

We'd been dating for eighteen months, and I don't know why but I'd not expected what came next. There'd been no conversations about the future beyond we both were businesspeople who fitted relationships into our work lives rather than the other way around. We could go weeks without seeing the other and yet it all worked beautifully. I'd thought I was happy.

Until my glass of champagne arrived with an engagement ring in it.

"Wh-what?" I looked at Patrick's gaze, his blue eyes slightly glazed with emotion. Only now did he display a hint of nervousness as he touched his lip, before rising from his seat, walking in front of me and dropping onto one knee.

"Ella Story, marry me."

I loved him. I genuinely did. But it wasn't the passionate, would die for you love I'd kept searching for. Did that really exist though or was it just a figment of my imagination?

Eyes were upon us, and he did make me happy...

"Yes," I said.

The other nearby occupants of the room cheered, and the ring was taken from the champagne and placed upon my finger.

I smiled. I accepted the congratulations of others, the free champagne, the kisses from my new fiancé.

But inside something didn't sit right with me, like the cold dread of having eaten something you think might give you food poisoning. Who put a ring in a drink, not in a box, having to fish it out with their fingers, then expected me to toast with the drink I felt was now tainted? Who proposed without any hint it was coming? Why was I feeling like this on what should be the happiest day of my life? It felt like dark shadows hid in corners of the restaurant, their gloom seeping into the atmosphere, into me, bringing sadness where there should be joy. I knew what the dark shadow was though. It was that tiny corner of my mind where thoughts of a vampire were stored.

Patrick and I celebrated with more champagne and went back to our room at the hotel. We made love and as he climaxed and folded me into his arms, Patrick said something so simple—something which should have alighted in me butterflies—but which instead sealed our fate.

He whispered the words next to my ear. "I can't wait to make you my wife and then make beautiful babies with you."

My reaction was visceral. Like I'd suddenly discovered I was allergic to my lover.

"I can't do this."

"Wh-what do you mean?"

"I can't do this. I can't marry you." I leapt out of bed, dressing quickly.

"Is it the kids thing? We can wait."

I began packing my belongings frantically into my case and Patrick ran over to me. His limp dick swung and I just physically recoiled. He saw my reaction.

"Goddamn it. I knew I was taking a risk. If I've ever mentioned the future, you've always changed the subject."

Had I? Had he actually mentioned our future and I'd just denied it all?

"But I love you, Ella, and I know you love me. You're just scared." He grabbed my hand and tried to guide me back to the bed. "Let's talk about this. Get things out in the open. There was another man, yes? Once upon a time in your past? We need to deal with this, maybe get a counsellor even. I know we'll be happy if we talk about whatever it is that's making you scared of commitment."

I sat on the bed, Patrick at my side, and I decided he should hear the truth.

"Yes, there was another man. Many, many years ago. He broke my heart and over the years I've thought one day another man would fix it." I gazed into Patrick's eyes. "I thought you would fix it."

"I can," he implored.

But I shook my head and began to remove the ring from my finger.

"Ella, don't do this," Patrick's voice cracked and I felt like the worst person in the world. But I'd have been the worst person to marry him when he could never be Beau.

"I'm sorry but it's over," I told him. I gathered my belongings and left a man devastated.

Arriving at the airport, I realised I did not want to go home to the Lakes. It no longer felt like home, but more a temporary residence, like student digs while you're at university. Now I craved the castle at Poplar. I needed to see it, to go back. I was done running, it was time to return.

Over the years, I'd laid claim to the now empty home of my father's and sold it and had also inherited all his wealth. I was rich beyond my wildest dreams and my plan was to see how much the current owner wanted for the castle. I would buy it myself. Maybe I couldn't have Beau, but I could have my perfect home.

I flew back to the U.K. and travelled to Poplar. As soon as my taxi began to trundle along the driveway, my stomach fizzed with excitement. I had to make this place mine. Would my mother still lie in the grounds, or would she now have been interred elsewhere? Did anything remain from before? The outside looked the same, but whatever the current occupants had done with the interior, I could make it what I wanted, even if that were to return it to how I remembered.

I paid the taxi driver and asked him to idle there while I saw whether I would be allowed entrance or not.

I was almost holding my breath by the time I pressed the doorbell.

I stood there, a cool breeze against my skin as I waited.

After a few minutes a butler answered the door.

"Yes?"

"I wish to see the current owner please?" I said confidently, although it was at that moment that I'd hoped Beau had stood there. I could no longer lie to myself. It wasn't just the house I wanted, I also desired to find the only man I'd ever loved heart and soul. "I have an offer to make them for the purchase of this castle," I quickly added, so that the butler knew I wasn't a salesperson of some kind.

The butler looked at me, intrigued and a little bemused.

"Please stay there for a moment. I will return." He closed the door in my face.

Standing on the doorstep, I huffed in frustration.

Now I wanted the place and wanted to find Beau again, every second wasted was annoying me.

Then the door opened and there he stood.

It took me a moment to find my voice, not only due to shock but also because my eyes were assessing every inch of him, marvelling that in all those years he'd not changed even a tiny amount.

"You never sold the damn house, did you?" I shook my head at him, not sure whether to kiss him or stake him.

His lip quirked. "Nope."

"I hate you."

"No, you don't." He folded his arms across his chest. "Tell me the reason you're back here."

"I came to buy the house."

"Really? Is that the only reason?"

My foot tapped on the floor. "Let me in. I'm not doing this on the doorstep."

"Hmmm, take off your shoe."

"Pardon?" I was in no mood to play stupid games and considered pushing past him. *Huh, as if you'd get past a wily super-strong vampire.* It was also when I remembered I had a taxi waiting.

I moved away from Beau and asked the driver to assist with getting my luggage on the driveway. Then I paid him and watched as his taxi faded into the distance. I basically stomped back over to Beau. "Can we go inside now?"

"Take off your shoe. If this shoe fits..." He revealed my old shoe. "...then I'll let you in."

"You are still as ridiculous I see as you were back then," I snapped, kicking off one heeled shoe and grabbing the shoe I'd left behind. I placed it on my foot. "See?"

"Just checking that even though you're now a woman of the world, you'd still obey my commands, because that's important, Ella."

"You talk in riddles. Now let me in for God's sake."

He moved to the side, and I waltzed in, now wearing odd shoes with different sized heels. "Please bring in my luggage," I ordered, and I heard him laugh, but he did so.

Leaving both shoes in the hallway, I began to walk up the stairs to head to what I hoped was still my suite of rooms. Happiness wrapped me like a warm blanket as I saw little of the castle had changed. Beau followed on behind until we reached the landing. Then he walked in the opposite direction.

"Where are you going?"

"To our room."

I placed a hand on my hip. "I came to buy the house, Beau."

He closed the space between us in seconds, yet so precise in his placement I'd not faltered on my own feet. His chest pressed against my breasts, his hand running through my hair as his face marvelled at touching it again. As if he couldn't believe it was real. "No, you didn't. Not really. You came home. That's what you did. You went out and saw the world and although you enjoyed it, you found it lacking against the small amount of world you'd found here with me. Now do you see why I had to let you go?"

"You're a dick."

His lip curled again. "I waited for you, Ella. There was no one else."

I paused, my fingers coming to my mouth as if to block the question I needed to know the answer to.

"Y-you didn't have children?"

"No, just years' worth's of cold showers." He chuckled.

My eyes widened.

"Ella, a vampire's desire can be satisfied with feeding. I remind you that I am not a human man, and how many times do I have to remind you that twelve years passes in a heartbeat for a cold one."

My mind transported back to the first time I'd met him.

"Uno freddo," I uttered. "You called me a cold

one."

"Co-incidence. I was talking back then about your delightful personality."

I ignored him, unconvinced by his argument. "Well twelve years does not pass in a heartbeat for a human woman. No human man has come close to making me feel how I felt with you."

"Of course not. I'm your soulmate, Ella," he scoffed.

"Then why did you send me away and waste all those years?" I demanded.

"You always would have wondered what life outside the castle could have been like. But it would have been full of your imagination and not reality. Because you'd have tied yourself to babies when you didn't really want them. You know why anyway. Yes, twelve years seems a long time now, but those years will eventually feel like—"

"The blink of an eye," I finished.

"Yes. Now come with me," he said, and grabbing my hand he walked me down to his own rooms. I relished the coolness of his hand in my warm one. I craved his touch beyond hand-holding, but for now it was a start.

Beau pushed open his bedroom door and there it was: a replica of my birdcage. But this version was carved in gothic black iron. It was exquisite. A replica, but much larger. Beau's bed was in the centre of it.

"You sleep in a cage?"

"Yes, but always with the door open, for in case you came home."

"But you desired children. Why did you wait?"

"Because I love you, Ella. I decided I would wait until you were past childbearing age before I mourned your loss and began to look anew. Yet I couldn't imagine it. I always kept hope that one day you'd come home."

"And I have."

"You have. But, Ella, now you must know this. If you're staying, I'm claiming all of you this time. The door on this cage will close every night. Your body will be mine. You will be mine. I'll be caging you, Ella. The true nature of a vampire is to possess."

I walked inside the cage.

"Show me," I commanded.

"Oh, I intend to. But first, you need to unpack, and have some sustenance. Then we have matters to discuss."

"I want your babies, Beau. I want all of you. Everything you have to give. I love you," I told him, becoming frustrated with the barriers he was still putting in place between us.

"You also need to be turned before any of that happens. So, unpack, refreshments, and then we retire to our suite, to *talk*."

I sighed. "Always so stubborn."

He laughed.

He may not have fucked me, but he couldn't stop kissing me and trailing his fingers over my body as if checking I was really there. We talked through the night and then his fingers and tongue claimed my body as they always had. But this time it was different. Though I longed for his cock, I knew that Beau Salinger belonged to me. His heart, his body, his essence. And the next day, he turned me into a vampire. Into his true mate.

Then he locked me in the cage.

He fed me over the next few days as all I felt was blood lust and pain. I rattled the cage to be freed, but I couldn't move the iron. And then the pain and thirst left me, and I felt myself again, albeit with much sharper senses.

Beau opened the cage door. "Come, my bride, we

shall walk the grounds of our home and you can see the place with fresh eyes."

It took me time to adjust, because colours were in sharper focus. As we walked towards my riverside bench, the greens of the trees looked intense, painted with every shade I'd ever seen on paint swatches. The sky was so very midnight, the stars looked like diamonds. I turned to look back at the castle and the moonlight was like an angelic beam upon the stonework.

Smiling, I took Beau's hand.

"Everything is so beautiful," I told him.

"Not as beautiful as you," he said.

He dropped to one knee as I stood next to the river and held out a box containing a ring.

"Moonstone," he explained. "Vampires don't marry in the traditional sense of the word. You are already my bride to me, but with this ring, I thee wed," he said. I held out my hand and he placed the ring on my finger.

And this time it felt utterly right.

"Now it's time you were mine completely," he said. "Are you ready?"

"Yes," I answered, and he spirited me back inside.

CHAPTER 17

BEAU

She'd returned. It had been the hardest thing to send her away, but I needed to know that given her choices in life, she still desired me. Every man she'd kissed and/or slept with had cut deep, but I was no innocent and I wanted Ella to have the world at her fingertips. Twelve years I'd kept in the background watching her become the woman she was now.

When she went to Paris and I saw Patrick place the ring on her finger, I'd left and come home. I'd thought she was lost to me. And then I'd answered the door and there she'd been.

And I knew. She was mine, for definite. For now, and for eternity.

I'd never had any intention of selling up. I'd been learning to invest money and had enough for the upkeep of the place. In time my investments would grow further. I was in no rush. As long as I could stay at Moonstone Castle and have Ella and children, I needed nothing further.

And now my vampire bride was in my arms and in our bedroom. I could make her mine completely. Could finally sink into her warm depths. Treat her as a strong vampire, not a frail human.

"Now I show you who I am and what I desire, Ella. I can only hope you enjoy it too. I'm sure you'll let me know if you don't." I arched a brow and received an eye roll in return.

Stepping inside the birdcage, I opened a drawer under the bed and took out a pair of hand restraints.

"Come, Ella," I beckoned. She followed my direction. "Strip for me," I commanded, and she did. A teasingly slow routine. As she lost the last piece of clothing, her panties, I grabbed her arm and pushed her back into the frame. I tied her hands to a thin bar above her head. Her breasts pushed out enticingly and I feasted on a stiffened peak. And then I bit down.

"Fuck, oh my, Beauuuuu," she moaned, as my vampire venom hit her system, mingling with her own. The pain would bring her pleasure. Blood dripped from her nipple, and I sucked it and then licked the wound closed.

I stood back, watching her against the frame, her eyes hooded and her desire spilling down her inner thighs.

"Beau, please," she begged.

"What would you like me to do?" I asked.

"Fuck me."

"Is that all? Tell me everything. Whatever you want me to do from now until I enclose you in my arms in that bed for our very first night as lovers."

I saw her chew on her lip, before a small, teasing smile bloomed in my direction.

"Fuck me. Cum in me. Give me your seed, Beau. Make me pregnant."

That was the moment I was truly and utterly gone for my vampire bride. She knew exactly how to play me. To torment me and delight me.

I brought her off with my tongue first, and then I uncuffed her and brought her down to the floor and onto our bed. Moving over her body I gazed down into her eyes. "You're mine, Ella."

Then I pushed inside her. Moving slowly, I kept my gaze on hers, and she locked hers on me. Slowly, I thrust in and out, and she began to match my rhythm, tilting her hips and driving me crazy. Faster and faster we moved together until I felt the tell-tale tingle in my cock, and then I bit down on Ella's neck.

We came together hard, her milking my cock as I climaxed inside her. It seemed like I could picture my seed flowing within her. I didn't want to waste a drop and as I withdrew from her, I quickly grabbed her ankles and swung her around to where the head of the bed was. Grabbing the cuffs, I fastened each ankle to a lower bar around the cage so that her pelvis was tilted up, resting against the pillows. She acquiesced without questions or complaints.

I knelt at the side of her. "I've barely wasted a drop of my spunk and I'm going to push everything I see inside you," I said. Her pink folds began to glisten afresh. "Does that turn you on, my sweet wife, me pushing my cum deep inside you?" My fingers began to plunge within her, and she thrust up to meet them.

"Yes, I want it all, your cum, your fingers, another orgasm," she demanded. "I mean, while I'm in this position, the least you can do is keep me entertained."

I kept her entertained all right. It was days before we left the room.

Epilogue

Ella

I bore six children. My first a daughter we named Snow after the weather of her birth. Then Dove arrived, named after the bird that settled on the windowsill as I birthed her. Isabel was next. We'd visited Italy and Beau wished to call her Bella, his beauty. I argued it was too close to my own name and so we settled on Isabel.

Then three sons. Phillipe, after the vampire doctor who helped deliver him when there were complications; Gene after Beau's father; and then finally the little boy who'd just been placed in my arms, Reid.

My husband stroked my hair, and kissed first my forehead, then my lips, and then the top of our son's head. The other children were being cared for by Iris who'd decided she was their 'Faerie Grandmother'.

"I think we did well on this bout of my fertility," Beau said, having kept me pregnant for the best part of five years. "I shall spend the next forty-five years giving you endless orgasms."

"And help with all these children we've had," I ordered.

"Always so bossy, my beautiful wife," he said, laughing.

I stared at our new son and then my husband. "I love you, Beau Salinger."

"And I love you, Mrs Salinger. Shall we bring in the other children?"

"Yes," I agreed. He went to fetch them, and returned carrying Gene, the other little ones rushing in alongside him.

And I looked at my husband and children and realised I could not have wished for a better happy forever after.

THE END

Snow Salinger is all grown up in the second paranormal fairy tale retelling.

Discover what happens when she encounters seven wolf shifters in *Sharing Snow*, a why choose/breeder romance out in September 2023.

To keep up on Andie's book releases, sales, and other news, join her mailing list and receive the Supernatural Dating Agency short story prequel *Dating Sucks*: geni. us/andiemlongparanormal

Musical Inspiration

The Lakes – Taylor Swift

Carolina – Taylor Swift

Sign of the Times – Harry Styles

About Andie

Andie M. Long lives in Sheffield, UK, with her long-suffering partner, her son, and a gorgeous Whippet furbaby.
She's addicted to coffee and Toblerone.

When not being partner, mother, or writer, she can usually be found wasting far too much time watching TikTok.

Andie's Reader Group on Facebook
www.facebook.com/groups/haloandhornshangout

TikTok and Instagram
@andieandangelbooks

Paranormal Romance By Andie M. Long

COMEDY

Sucking Dead

Suck My Life – available on audio.

My Vampire Boyfriend Sucks

Sucking Hell

Suck it Up

Hot as Suck

Just My Suck

Too Many Sucks

Also available in paperback and bundle of books 1-3 available.

Supernatural Dating Agency

The Vampire wants a Wife

A Devil of a Date

Hate, Date, or Mate

Here for the Seer

DIDN'T SEA IT COMING

PHWOAR AND PEACE

ACTING CUPID*

CUPID FOOL*

Books one to six also on audio.

Series available in paperback.

Series bundles of books 1-3, and 4-6 available.

Acting Cupid and Cupid Fool were previously released as Cupid Inc, but have been extensively rewritten and now form part of Supernatural Dating Agency and...

the series will continue... in 2023.

HEX FACTOR

HEAVY SOULS

WE WOLF ROCK YOU

SATYRDAY NIGHT FEVER

Also in paperback. Complete series ebook available.

OTHER PARANORMAL ROMANCE

Filthy Rich Vampires – Reverse Harem

Royal Rebellion (Last Rites/First Rules duet) – Time

Travel Young Adult Fantasy

Immortal Bite – Gothic romance

Printed in Great Britain
by Amazon